Flesh of the Peach

Helen McClory

**FREIGHT
BOOKS**

First published 2017

Freight Books
49–53 Virginia Street
Glasgow, G1 1TS
www.freightbooks.co.uk

ISBN 978-1-911332-25-1
eISBN 978-1-911332-26-8

Typeset by Freight in Plantin
Printed and bound by Bell and Bain, Glasgow

the publisher acknowledges investment from
Creative Scotland toward the publication of this book

Why does tragedy exist? Because you are full of rage. Why are you full of rage? Because you are full of grief.

— Anne Carson, *Grief Lessons: Four Plays by Euripides*

To all the unlikeable women in fiction
and outwith it.

She stood out on the observatory of the Empire State Building in failing light, felt delicate and underslept, and waited for something decisive to occur. Maybe she'd be there until closing. Did they close this place? Every night the top of the building glowed different colours. Beacons for the various dread causes. And maybe out of cause-kinship, every night, all through the night, they let fools gather to acknowledge their own.

Sarah's causes? They were slimy, incriminating, broken, partial. She rummaged in her bag for a ginger sweet. Sucked down on sticky fire, and stared out across the city. I am alone, she thought, who the fuck could aid me but me? She pulled down the sunglasses from the top of her head. That helped. You should always at least have a bit of poise. It wasn't that she particularly cared if tourists noticed she had been crying. Just that she was fond of her projections. The kind of person who went to her solitary bed in light makeup and skimpies in order to present fierce aspect. To herself, to anything in the world that might be leering in her window.

It is strange the ease in which you can enact projections. Flip down the shades and step into another life. A gilded life. It could happen, it happened. As if on cue, camera flashes crashed against her raw skin. Longhair swish. She bared her teeth for pictures taken by strangers. The milling crowd jostled her, craning towards the skyscrapers and calling out, that's the Hudson! Look, a helicopter! Happy enough. A murmur glut passing through the channel of her body.

Sarah looked beyond the silver of the bars. It was beautiful. All the city in the early evening was lavender and greys of rare distinction, twenty miles worth of it touched by haze. After a while Sarah mumbled to the bars a prayer of falling. How to fall through a cage three metres high. She would have to shred herself. What a scene. People lingered waiting for dusk to flicker into night, others left quickly. She made tiny movements with her hands. She listened to voices detaching from the stream and threading away back inside. Are we doing this then, she asked herself.

The question was vague because she herself was vague. It becomes a lyric in a city like this one. Sarah's lover Kennedy had just severed ties. Kennedy had been everything for a while there. A streak of lightning, against an otherwise drab sky. A rooted New England New Yorker married to a man who sounded, in his calls and written messages, limply vile. And violent now. Which was the preferable option – violence done to you by another or the violence you do to yourself? Sarah felt she was standing on that other ragged side of love, where gravity wore thin the edges of the body. You have to ask yourself the most ridiculous questions. Do you want to live. Is your living a worthwhile act. Do you want an extra shot of caramel. Are you going to be able to pick your teeth right out of your jaw. Who the hell is keeping note, at any rate.

Sarah licked her lips and the wind chilled them. Her teeth pinched her tongue. Yes she still had lips, teeth. She still had her silky black hair, her best treasure. No falling today. Instead, I am going to leave, she thought. She unwrapped another ginger chew, slid it in her mouth and pondered this decision. Fuck it, I ruined this whole city for myself, but I have plenty more. This is a very American thing to do.

She gazed through the bars with what she assumed was an empty expression. She turned to face the crowd in the same way. Her mother was dead back home in England, that was the other thing. Finally, after a slow dance with cancer. And long after their relationship had died. The idea of going back to Cornwall to help with the estate and put on a show in front of her aunt and cousin made her feel unsanitary. It grubbied her.

Sarah opened and closed her fists in an effort to jog her blood pressure. She felt the problem in terms of altitude sickness or else chafed nerves, and when she wasn't leaning on something her vision trembled. But how lucky she was, her mother had left all those millions to her. Just put it in a clean little envelope, Madam Barrister, thank you very much, like a neat towelette slipped alongside the balled-up pink knickers from last night.

She unwrapped another ginger. Sugar rush helped, fire helped. Working the wad against her back teeth, almost choking herself. Two paths had emerged. One home across the pond, and another unseen in the American interior beckoning her. It was an easy choice, all considered.

You could be on Browne family land for a mile and not know it. And to get into the Warne itself, you had to trust that bone-rattler of a flagstone road to take you down on your bike through steeply-sloping pasture. Ditch your ride at an odd angle, in among the yews. Ignore the main gate and follow the old brick wall until it leads to the chipped red door with the only brass sign left in the place, saying 'Warne: walled garden', and that's where you slipped in, if you had the key. And Sarah did.

Brownes never used the front entrance unless for a guest or other strange event.

So, you go into the walled garden and are immediately confronted by the sight of the Warne itself, planted at the end of the stretch: a yellow-painted mansion in the eighteenth-century fashion. A fair demonstration of farmer-squire wealth, with sagging drains and ivy and a crooked dovecot in need of painting and doves.

You can't see it that close to the wall, but sharp to the right is a short brambled walk down to the creek. Silver and black and wide. A town across from it higgledy in the early morning winter light. And out beyond that, the English Channel extending past the headland of the town. The channel that goes to France directly south, or straight on across the Atlantic, till America.

The gardens had been laid out in Italianate style and devastated by the twentieth century. Old English pears and medlars still fanned, neglected, against the brickwork. Later, Maud and Selene Browne somewhat cleared the grounds of brush and wet slime. Sometimes the long beds are overcome with roses and other flowers. Roses like the roses of sleeping beauty, all flesh and leggy, their sudden, green-spotted blooms hinting at dreams of sex.

You had to duck the briars, following the stone path,

watching for the choked pond that you, in your fifteenth year, dredged and stocked with fish. The fish all eaten by a heron the next spring. Shall we say there is a thin ice on the pond, and the fish are gone.

You then get up to the back door, the kitchens. And there are herbs of all sorts; sweet cicely, borage, winter savory. Mint like a rebuke when you jam a cache of it under your tongue.

You get that heavy green door open and step inside on the indented stones. The door clicks shut or thuds behind like the door of a country church. You read that line in a poem, read it over until the meaning grew to encompass the great still house.

Here you stop on the threshold and peer into the dimness, listening for kindly ghosts, or cousin Lucy. The damp pervading against the fire in the kitchens. The only dry rooms, westerly facing, up on the second floor, where the two women and two girls would camp at night.

But you remain on the threshold, the door never opens, never shuts behind. You are outside, and you can go no further. And this outsideness, the jags of memory, fit into your skull to be lodged there, for however long.

In a day Sarah was to leave the city. She ripped open an envelope while climbing the two sets of stairs to her apartment, and carefully took out a printed booklet that detailed her two and a half days of travel on the Greyhound bus. A stark black list of city names, some famous she'd absorbed from passive contact with American culture, some that had never made it through. And at the foot of the list, Santa Fe. In Northwest New Mexico. Up beyond it was the cabin her mother had apparently used as a summer home, and likely a touring base when she was off trying to flog her tacky canvases of misty Olde England. Moving to the cabin would take her two thousand miles away from Kennedy. Two thousand more on top of the Atlantic to separate her from the family pile. A good start.

Sarah had purchased herself some leaving gifts, including a water canteen patterned with arabesques and a bright yellow sundress. Twenty-six caffeinated nutrient bars. A landslide of gingers. She stood with her bags in her apartment, a single green-walled room.

She placed the newly purchased dress so that it lay across the bed in a pool like sunshine. Beautiful thing with one long wrinkle in the fabric. It was the most important item for that long moment. Sarah had tried for an age to be an artist but all that had left her with was a passion for surfaces. Beauty in colour and form. In the image associations of this particular yellow shade: of sunshine, butter, primrose, spring. She was going to dress from now on for a beautiful life. Keep saying those words to yourself. It sounds naïve but that is one way to choose to exist. As a polished stone skipped across the harshness of things.

The room smelled as it always did – of Sunday, of old Pear's soap and toast crusts. Sarah turned on the A/C and lowered the blinds until the room was dim, then removed her clothes.

She showered in the windowless bathroom where the only noise was of water, lulling. It was a good idea not to let herself linger, as it might result in bright blue scales emerging from her soft pruney flesh. Mermaid armour. A story Lucy had told her of Roseland sirens who had abandoned their lovers and swum out beyond the St Mawes harbour. In downtime between sailor murderings they would occupy themselves in combing their wet green hair with the forks and knives picnickers left behind. If you swam three times in the creek at high tide, that brought on the mermaid disease. Or if you lurked too long in the bath. Though it had been years since she believed the story, Sarah ran her hands all over her skin to make sure it was still as it should be, sensitive and supple beneath her fingernails.

She got out and dried herself slowly. Whatever the last few months had done to her she was still in her own body. You can sift yourself free of a place. It's possible to be delicate and fierce at once. Put on a yellow dress and push back against that regular thought that all you are came from a terrible moment at seventeen. Push that back, and keep pushing. The dress holds you in, ever so softly. A sunny freckle on her shoulder, a thumbprint-sized bruise at her wrist, a little mid-palm scar. These graffiti were her self-made maker's marks. Her vanity was limited and very specific.

Sarah went to get a cup of tea thinking that to stay whole, to be wounded but to manage, that was the point. Easy enough if you had energy. She fished the tea bag from the hot water, wrung it out and tore it open above the bin, mashing the dank leaf bits through her fingers. That charming smell of tannins and comfort. She would miss these. Stocks were down to the last box of decent English tea. So you are not going to kill yourself, or go home for the wretch of a funeral, but you will have to live without some comforts. So you are going to run off to live in that vague and vaguely terrifying America-outside-New-York and be the best possible version of yourself.

She took her suitcase into the middle of the floor and began to fold clothes and other pieces within. The end result was neat, albeit a little sad. After that she sat cross-legged on her bed with a netbook on her knees. She blew and sucked at her tea and did an image search for the six acres with a wooden cabin in the Valle Grande of New Mexico.

Free spontaneous hiking;
Wilderness elk hunt;
Good campsite practice.

The pictures scrolling by were of an undulating golden plain and pine forested mountains. Not, as Sarah had thought, flat scrubland and blistering sands. She had hoped for those tall cactuses that were so aloof, hoped to be living in a landscape harsh and scoured clean. She was disappointed, but this was still unlike the wet salty southern coast of Cornwall. It was enough of a disconnection. Sarah opened the lawyer's email. A scan of the cabin deeds had been included. The deeds to the Warne too. She quickly closed the files.

She sat staring a while. Tapped her teeth hard against her teacup, pushed at the bruise on her wrist. Someone upstairs screamed an epithet of high colour. Then muffled crying. Sarah suddenly thought of Viking berserkers who in their fury would bite down on the edges of their shields. The mug had to be washed, then into the suitcase with everything else. She tried not to think of axes breaking teeth, and of the shock of unwanted blood. Her mouth hurt, and she had to feel her face to check for damage.

You find the edges and you find the harmed places within the edges. It had been in Kennedy, and all that embroilment. She had wanted warmth and to be harmed. To feel beloved and stung. She had wanted to blister from love, not to have to flee. But the fact was that nothing tied her now to this berserk, sweltering city, certainly not in that other bed across town now filled with Kennedy and her wankrag husband and only traces of Sarah's ghost.

She kneeled on the floor putting the last few items away. Cry, damn you. You can't lose your job crying at home. You can't inconvenience anyone. To weep hot, private, ugly tears. She pulled at her hair, the tears would not come. She covered her face and nearly laughed at herself. This is the beginning. This is your new dress and your ticket to the West.

4

Four hours left. Sarah sat in her hollowed apartment in her loose travel clothes. Soon she'd be gone and maybe only the neighbour's bulldog would remember. And even then, it would just be the smell of her hands as it had licked her. She was thinking about how she'd sat outside on the steps of the fire escape on one of innumerable summer nights, waiting on a call from her lover. It was a little after midnight, and occasionally at that time desperation would draw Kennedy to the phone. Hope is the thing with barbs that never ever lets you go. Or is that loneliness.

Out on that fire escape, August, the streetlights clung to her and the skyline of Manhattan shone through the leaves. Nothing was real but Sarah. And the clothes that weighed against her skin. She always forgot that nights could be warm, too. This was the week before her mother had died. Back then she'd still had a semblance of ordered life, her lover across town, her moral centre a sun below the horizon, and an outline of her history setting out how each step led brusquely onto the next.

She had left home when she was seventeen.

She had never been back.

She had never really left.

She had done so well in the local school.

She had hidden at the front of the class.

She had been privileged to live in a mansion.

She had contracted bronchitis every February.

She couldn't speak because every word she spoke was privilege, she couldn't stop herself speaking because she was lonely, hopeful. She was the daughter of a famous, popular artist. An unacknowledged daughter of a Japanese-American art lover.

She had been painted many times as a child, but her mother changed her hair from the slink of black it was to fluffy chick blonde in every cottage row and misty riverbank scene.

Skip some steps.

She had left that all long ago and was different now.

She was Sarah New York City.

Back in the empty apartment, Sarah sat hope-filled and looked inside her suitcase again. One chambray shirt. One pair of jeans. That ripple of sunshine. What else did cowgirls need? Black and blue underwear. Winter boots. Keys to the cabin. Hair ties. These transitional periods before solidity reforms you again, all temporarily. Breathing the air that comes up from inside a luggage case. How it is a promise continually renewed. But on this occasion, a promise of what? Well, don't be premature. Hope and its hooks growing into tumbleweed.

5

'What's your order, K?'

'You don't have to get up. They come to the table.'

Sarah frowned at the menu. Kennedy picked at her nails. She had them done in a parlour in the LES and had told Sarah the name of it. Was it the one with a hand holding a rose on the outside, Sarah had asked. It was better to humour Kennedy, but some part of her resisted. Kennedy was distracted that evening. Later she'd drop the bomb that her husband had found out. Implied, that she had told him. She picked at her nails and her eyes kept flicking towards her bag, to the phone inside it lighting up. Every half hour, lighting up.

'Are we friends, would you say?' Sarah asked, at the tail end of some comment about frenemies at work, looking up and smiling nervously. There was a trellis of vines overhead. Open to the night sky above. That luxury.

'No, honey, you know we aren't that.'

Sarah felt for the edge of the table. A waiter appeared. She looked at him while Kennedy studiously did not. The waiter had a thin, crooked neck, with wispy blond hairs on his Adam's apple.

'Could I please have a gin and tonic. With a slice of orange?' she asked.

'I'll have a vodka tonic,' said Kennedy.

When the waiter had gone, Kennedy did the usual thing of chastising Sarah for asking instead of ordering. 'You'd think you'd know how. You're so weird when you do it that kinda little girl way.' But she did smile. Fidgeting her wedding ring as if she might take it off.

After the drink they went to a hotel overlooking Central Park they had pre-checked on the bedbug registry. There they plied themselves with smuggled-in red wine, watched porn paid for by Sarah, and fucked discretely. That was the correct label. Sex that was distinct from all other facets of their lives and personalities. Only their bodies were involved, glossy with sparks and sweat.

Afterwards Kennedy turned on the TV and stared at a weather report. Count a beat of ten. Then told Sarah that her husband had found out. 'So we're done now.' An unblinking shrug. 'I like you but hey.' And after Sarah had finished being silent, Kennedy turned off the TV and said, 'Let's get some sleep, okay hun?' And pulled on her underwear and turned away.

In the morning very early Sarah had left, walked stiffly out of the plush foyer of the hotel. Thinking, I know this place from a movie, but which one. She was almost at 27th and 3rd before she realised, oh, *Home Alone 2*. Sarah blanked on where she had watched the film, or when, or how many times. She picked through the scenes she could remember: Central Park across the street, steam vents, and a mass of glittery Christmas lights. She walked faster, thinking of it, and deliberately steering herself back to the images and nothing else. A children's film, it was cute. Someone in an attic, feeding pigeons. Now she remembered. Sarah, nine, watched the video, lying on her stomach spooning heated-up tinned macaroni into her mouth. And so she walked hunched, hands in her pockets, through a New York winter from 1993. Though it was not then or there but a hot morning in summer in the second decade of the twenty-first century post-everything and she could not contain the city like a movie could. Only two cameras set in her head. Close one eye, close the next. Sarah had stopped in the middle of the road. But only for a second. A car horn beeped, shaking her out from under herself.

'What the hell do you want from me,' she yelled at the cab.

At work in the coffee shop in Union Square. Sarah had been dreamy, fearful, spilling things, overheating the milk. On a mandated break, she had checked her phone. There was a message from Kennedy that said: do NOT check ur voice mails.

Seven new voicemails.

Hi Sarah, this is Marc. I don't believe we've met but you know my wife—

You gonna pick up your phone Sarah or am I gonna have to keep—

Look, I'd like to talk to you, I know you're out with Kennedy right now, right fucking now, I think you owe me that much—

Pick up your fucking phone, Sarah—

Sarah… Sarah, you fucking whore, it's all right, Sarah you cu—

I don't know why you'd think this is okay, listen, I'm gonna make myself heard—

You have to listen to three or four seconds before you hit delete, otherwise the machine won't let you.

Anyway, so this is Marc, again, it's twelve of six in the morning. I'm a lot calmer than I was, you know? So… maybe give me a call back. Or don't. Or, you know, I'll fucking shoot you in your fucking – or whatever. Have a lovely morning, Sarah.

Sarah put her forehead down on the sticky break room counter. She felt grit embed. Someone walked in and turned on their heels and walked right back out. This was awkward. But what else was she supposed to do? There wasn't room for a table, there wasn't room for her to pace nor anything to kick over. So she pinned herself down against that counter with her hands on the back of her head as if being arrested. The phone in front of her, a spent weapon. Outside the room, the scouring sounds of coffee being made. Her face felt hot and then numb. Some new shuffling behind her. Sarah, you okay milady? A mumbled, yes, will be. After a minute she got up and breathed as if she had been under water for a while. Then picked up her phone and went online to check her emails. Her eyes didn't work too well, but her fingers were real enough, her own short, coffee-smelling white-speckled nails. One new email:

Dearest Cousin
Your mother sadly passed away last night.
Maud was comfortable, she asked after you.
She said she wanted to hold your hand.
The service will be next week.
—Lucy

And that was how Sarah lost her job. And the voicemails continued for three days. And all she was was an émigré deadmother wifefucker in pieces, spines, vibrating at an awful screeching pitch.

From there, to the Empire State building. From there, her pieces sent out to be hopeful and reformative – somewhere other.

Sarah walked to the bus terminus. Memories were warping around her as she passed through the humid city. She acknowledged the warp, and determined it would end when she stepped on to the bus.

Memories of being in the Sixth Street garden, sitting by the koi pool, looking down at the juicy bodies swimming in the unreflectant water. And there Kennedy was, for the first time. Putting up her fine blonde hair while talking on the phone. Talking dirty, though Sarah couldn't hear. A cackle of laughter, a glimmer to the lips.

Kennedy's lipbalm, a tin of organic beeswax, smelling like boiled strawberries. Sarah rolling the goo between her fingers. This was what sex with Kennedy felt like. Would feel like. There was no end. She must try, though.

Not thinking about Kennedy in ruffled underwear practicing winking at her and never managing to keep the other eye open. Not thinking of how they drove to Long Island and fought on that beach and all the drive back, about him noticing the bill for swordfish from the seafood stand and gas and Kennedy's pale eyes empty while her mouth roared and the grass crouched by the sea and under the trees like a country that would be her country, if only she could stay.

Sarah blinked. She had reached the boarding point for the bus deep underground, and set her luggage down. The low, tiled space was coldly sweating dirt. All of New York below ground is simultaneously itself and the drab platform to Hell on hot days. The idea of mud-grey rats with greased fur. Their wormy rat-theatre productions conducted over knots of pretzel chucked on the tracks. The idea of a smeared pestilence on chrome and doorways. Subway stops so thick with diseased air, you want to run back out and drag everyone up to the surface with you.

A man, or the shadow of a man in the bus station booth took her luggage and weighed it, muttered some questions: knives, explosives, guns? And handed it back slapped with a label for the end point, two thousand miles away. From here on in, everything would travel in a clean, straight line, over even roads, under a bright new American interior sky.

Some more of Sarah's history. Sarah when young: she would eat her meals in the Warne's broken greenhouse. She would touch moss with her lips to see how it felt. She would pretend to have powers. She would pretend to see the Virgin Mary down at the creek and talk to her about art. She would retreat indefinitely and draw the Warne roses and later lie and say she had given up drawing at all.

She had stared at her Aunt Selene when Aunt Selene was drinking in the library. Her aunt called her a cunt and told her to cunting toddle off now. She had taken Aunt Selene's alcohol stash from the unused servant's toilets down to the creek and threw some of the bottles in. She had not been terribly satisfied by this.

She had taken the family cat down to the river when she was twelve but burdened with guilt had set him on the edge of the river, and he had flicked his tail in the water and looked at her, mouthing words of his confusion. She had eaten some of his cat biscuits as punishment and then was sick. She had a few memories of such rash actions and self-punishment after.

She stopped going to church when she was nineteen. She didn't stop talking to the Virgin, even after she herself was not.

She had broken a pane of greenhouse glass after a fight with her mother. She had brought the piece of glass into the house and taken it upstairs. She had taken it upstairs with intent, up to the bed where her mother lay sleeping. Hand palm up on the pillow next to her face. She had cut her mother's right hand with the jagged glass as she slept. Cut the meaty part of the palm below the thumb, knowing it might sever the muscle there. She had seen the blood on the pillow and her mother wake fearful and screeching. She had hated herself in a rich, evocative way.

She had left to go to art school.

At art school, and her string of failures. Mediocre art, teachers who knew whose daughter she was. Of that execrable sentimentalist Maud Browne. Sarah couldn't hide her mother inside her mouth, and in London she had no sense of touch. Her mouth disobeyed and her eyes were dull and her body leaked ink, externalised as bruise. There was a time before she had settled into her bisexuality, a period of self-deception where she pretended to be a heterosexual pretending to be a lesbian. Pretending that art was all she wanted to fire her. Letting art become ungraspable, and bodies slippery, and her own flesh. In London, Sarah was always ill, but never made a doctor's appointment. Said yes to letting the body sink into itself, like a body weighted in a flooded quarry. When she dropped out, there was little fanfare and no ticker tape parade.

She lost several years to sales assistant work, folding tee-shirts and gazing at the door, it was one grand and silent carnival. She might even have drawn a few times. And had sex a few times, and fingered twenty pound notes as she put them safely into the till, and was devoid for whole hours of wishes. That was it, really. That was Sarah.

Now check again, what was she? Not much as yet. A bundle on the Greyhound. The bundle hid its head under a hoody and narrowed its eyes at the view.

The bus was caught in a snarl before the Lincoln tunnel. Sarah gazed out the window at a man with a crooked yellow umbrella still up as he stared into the honking traffic. He was just waiting, in his old suit. Until he was gone.

It was Christmas day at the Warne, '97 or '98. Sitting in the library by the fire and hoping for snow that never came. The clouds a low matt acrylic, but not spitting out so much as a single flake. Everyone in the house had eaten a fine lot of clementines. They sat among the peels, holding glasses of brandy. Lucy had eaten six chocolate truffles, and Sarah had spooned away most of a helping of Christmas pudding. 'We must go on a walk in the fresh air,' Maud had said. 'We must. Off to the barrow. Not too far, and just enough strange.'

Maud worried about the Warne a lot, in those days. It was always threatened with having to be sold off. The roof was always caving in, or leaking, or infested with rot. That had become the story: we must save the mansion from falling into the hands of the bankers. We must save the mansion from falling into the creek. These were boom years in other parts of the country, but not with the Brownes. Maud reminded them it was not for many other people either. Maud had been rich, briefly, in the 1980s, but something had slipped, and the money was gone. It was only later, at the turn of the century, that her horrid twee paintings would start to sell again in big numbers and the coffers, whatever coffers were, choke on the ill gains.

Aunt Selene kept the wolf back somewhat, working in Plymouth, doing something very boring she never talked about. Selene in thick woollen blankets swigging brandy, with her hair in a bun. When she was drinking, she always had it up. And the old paintings of dead relatives had all been sold, many of the eighteenth and nineteenth century landscapes too, gone to a museum or to private collectors neither her mother or aunt would name. These objects vanished from the walls, discoloured rectangles left in their places. That was why Maud started painting again: for something to hang up, to add cheer against the old flock paper.

Maud was always trying to cheer. She would let no one admit their failures. Here, Sarah drew a circle around her mother. The dyed brown hair in a chignon, the boho cardigans overlain with flinty statement jewellery jangling at her chest. Her thin, diseased body and her careful laugh. Home since October, destined to be carted off yet again by the leukaemia in July. Her owlish and watery eyes had given little away.

The four of them staggering up the frosty hill to the plateau.

'We may have sold a bugger load of it off,' said Maud, marching, wheezing, 'but remember you can't rid a place of its history, not one bit, just by passing it on to someone else to keep. In fact, everything absolutely depends on the willingness to share.'

The barrow stood ahead of them, three feet tall and a table of stone, low and immobile. The clifftop road ran right by it, separated only by a fringe of grass. It had been there with its plated sides, under the leaden sky, for two thousand years.

Not far off in another field was a circle of standing stones commonly called the Dancing Men, a corruption of danse maen – 'stone dance'. In the other direction, a late-night shop that sold the Brownes their emergency pints of milk and tins of macaroni. Sarah was feeling queasy from the brandy and exercise, and cold and foolish. She determined to live in the here-and-now, not the here-and-then, airy-fairy like.

'Where we are now is on a ley line,' Maud said, 'a point of fluidity, by which we can navigate the constellations and count the days, predict certain astrological events.'

'You mean, astronomical events,' Sarah said, 'things that happened in the sky. Not predicting fortunes and that rubbish.'

Sarah hiding her deck of Tarot cards under her bed. Sarah

and Lucy playing a game of flick-the-book to find divining sentences. Writing these down in THE JOURNAL of L & S DO NOT TOUCH!! next to cut-outs of Leonardo DiCaprio and Jarvis Cocker.

'Ah, this smart daughter of mine,' Maud said.

'What do proper, normal families do at Christmas?'

'Not everyone celebrates, Sarah.'

'No mum, I know,' said Sarah.

Some more talk. And then placatory they each put their thin hands on the cold barrow roof. We're going to get stuck here by the frost and lose a finger, she thought. Then thought of the bones under them. The likely trove of muddy, gleaming coins.

Touching the barrow roof the veins in her hand ran with ancient ice and the cold spread upwards like an incantation expelling itself, mute.

'Nothing we do, in our brief time, will have the permanence of this,' said Maud.

And then of course you feel stupid, even as the spell is casting itself through you.

And fifteen years later, stupid that the memory still sings in you, as if the years had not intervened.

'Ma'am, would you mind if I closed the curtain?'

'Hmm? No, if you want.'

The woman in the seat next to hers reached over and hid the farewell vista behind a fold of blue canvas. Thin, pale creature with her hair in braids. The face in profile looking a little off, like something from a medieval bestiary. Like an exotic animal the artist had never seen and yet enthusiastically attempted to render.

The bus started off again, into the white-tiled tunnel. The coach shuddering and clanking into New Jersey, and all hours beyond, that sort of destiny.

9

On went the Greyhound, blundering down a Pennsylvanian highway. It was a drab day and the road was beset by scrawny trees dusty with exhaust. Showing through, beyond, was American suburbia. Too large a concept. You get an idea from the old sitcoms but of course those take place on a stage and there is dark beyond, and a man with a wire in his ear flips the switch to the applause sign. Someone pats a hand, delivers their aphorism, and everyone laughs.

Sarah, to distance herself from this, flicked through her magazine. She had thought to pick up something on home renovation and had chosen poorly. Linen-dressed children clutching sprigs of fresh, ribboned lavender. On the next page a room with only a giant stone pot of falling water, catchment area beneath strewn with water-lilies, their white roots trailing like the combed-out beards of goats.

One picture of a room with a high ceiling and dirty flock walls, scuffed mantelpiece, reminded her of her Cornish home, of her kin. A house of women, her mother and aunt, her cousin. The library with the bay windows, the cold studio, the broken statuary, the brick-walled orchard. Those kinds of details, that peeled-paint opulence. But the bay windows were mould-spotted at the edges from the rain. The damp touched your throat. The log books with the names of the war dead, and empty greenhouses speaking of the drained family, of servants. Now too long ago to be mourned and yet remaining in the ledger, and the ledger kept safe as if anything could be done at all to mitigate the loss.

When the money had started to rush back in from the paintings, Sarah was already gone. She scowled at the authentic faked dying luxury in the magazine. Where to even fucking start.

Sarah thought often of class. Of where she, her family, fitted. Not clear cut, despite the generational home. The mother half-there, the aunt slouched in the pantry picking at dinner rolls snarling, it's my peace and quiet time, sweety. Yes, just like in Ab Fab but puffy and rural real abusive and no off switch. Cousin Lucy who taught Sarah how to add tea to top up a raided brandy bottle, water as the equivalent for gin. How to drink tomato juice and eat comb honey with toast to ease a hangover.

Nostalgia was like a vine, strangling her, sickly-scented. Maybe a plastic vine. Maybe a vine strung through with fibre optics, transmitting bits of something all the time. Interference. Glitch.

Where are you from then, Sarah? Americans did not know what Cornwall was at all. In her own mind, the dynamics of class, place, Cornishness and Englishness were jumbled. If she was now American, always having been technically half-American, though that thought gave her a biting, hollow feeling inside, then it was more convoluted still.

Sarah packed her mouth with ginger sweets. The trees moved forwards and enmeshed. No more suburbia beyond the window. Just Sarah and the other passengers on the bus leaning against the glass, hunkered. Until after two hours the woodscape began to break open. Sarah put in her headphones and listened to a vintage mixture that sugar-glazed everything she looked at. The road and its hypnotic edge of white line, white line, break, turn off.

Now it was into the Appalachian mountains, golden early afternoon. Sarah, sealed up tight and carried swiftly onwards. The trees high, above pocket meadows. Twinned silos. A little brown farmhouse with a steady look.

What she would spend her money on

She would shift lands as the fancy took. It would be a winter's night in the top or bottom of the world. It would be night in Rakiura, say, or by the shores of the Bering Sea, on the Aleutian Islands. Evocative names are to be found on the peripheries. She would have the luxury of vertigo from staring up at the unpolluted stars.

There would be a bird of prey flying low behind her, tied to her wrist by a cord of leather. When she was rich, she would bring a clan of keeling beasts wherever she went. Red wolves. Scaly pangolin that clutched at her fingers with their claws and tails. She would build towers full of machines powered by sunlight, or keep books that have no siblings. The unique would be hers. She would seek to harm no one, to be good.

She would set a glass tile in the soil whenever she was kind. One day be able to walk barefoot to every familiar place down a one-foot high, river-like road of the glass, letting the routes accrue. Her bird screaming and her own mouth loose and appearing without pain.

10

They sat on the beach waiting for each silver wave to come in. It was July under a molten sun, and boredom was slapped all over them, their skins glistened with it. The long dune grasses heavily tossed their blades. Lucy and Sarah's bikes lay off in the warm sand. Their bags at their feet. Out in the bay, two boys on white and red longboards were waiting for the unlikely waves to come in. The sound of the lazy channel waters fizzling against the shore.

'He won't talk to me,' said Sarah, 'you remember what he was saying to Jon about me. About my dad. What was it? "I heard he was a yakuza boss, duh, better not touch a hair on her head"? I fucking do not like him, thanks.'

'Well, yeah. He's a racist little shit. But look at him,' Lucy answered, breathing out theatrically. One of the boys paddling, the other missing. Under water. A tanned leg upwards.

'He's just a dot from here, a dot with brown on the top.'

'Nah. You need glasses. He's well fit.'

'If you like him that much, you go and talk to him. He's such a dickhead.'

'He wears his dickhead on the inside,' Lucy said.

'Yep. Where nobody sees but us.' Sarah rolled onto her stomach. 'Why don't we drown boys more? I could swim up and get him before he could blink.'

Lucy said nothing.

'Well, what I'm trying to say is I don't want to pull anyone who is stuffed with knobs.' Her blue cartoon beach towel had scrunched up underneath her, exposing areas of her skin to the sand. Under her summer dress, in her knickers, another towel soaked up clots of blood. Lucy the same.

'That's fair.'

'Do you think Mum and Aunt Selene will still be angry at me

when we get back?' Some crime committed, some slight. They were numerous and unforgiveable. Maud usually dismissed them with short, cold cruelty. Selene spat and yowled. Both eventually forgot.

'Yeah,' said Lucy, 'they'll probably send you away to Granny's again.'

'That'll be right. How long do we have to wait till they aren't going to murder me for no reason?' Sarah drew a face in the sand, crossed the sand-eyes out.

'Pthh,' said Lucy. Their mothers were hopeless. 'I fancy a 99 in a bit. Do you have any money?' she asked after a moment.

'Seventy-five pence? No, a pound seventy-five. You can have it. Lucy, Mum and Selene are just stupid idiots. I actually hate them,' said Sarah.

Sarah so angry then, all the time. Anger that was murky and rich. Not like the cold, compulsive anger of later on in London.

Lucy picked a piece of shell from her arm. The ends of her loose hair curled into the sand. Grains suspended there. She pushed up her bony feet and slid them into her unlaced trainers. The movement achieved with the least amount of effort. Sarah was impressed.

Where was Lucy, what was Lucy, any more?

'Are we going to talk to them?' Lucy pointed vaguely out to sea. 'Are we getting an ice cream or going home or what? It's up to you.'

'Don't put me in charge,' Sarah said.

'Mum's such a dick too. Her and Maud,' said Lucy. 'I think we should stay out all night. We've got the sleeping bags. That'll do. Just need some provisions.'

'Okay. I've got a Blue Riband somewhere. I could do with something to drink.'

'Lashings of ginger beer,' said Lucy.

'Fuck off. Hmm. But what if they come over and bother us?' Sarah pointed towards the surfers. Towards France across the sea.

'No one's going to bother us. Let's cross the inlet up there, get some shelter from the wind.'

And now you remember cuffing the sand off, and the way the sun began going down as you both stared at the residue of it on the water. And how there were rabbits on the hill, and you and your cousin chased them. And how late on you got nastily chilled and swore at each other, but mostly at everyone else, and fell asleep huddled, and woke up to the beautiful dawn with a film of dew on the outside of your sleeping bag. How Maud and Selene had not noticed. Bottles lined up against the sunlit kitchen counter, and one of them tipped over dribbling wine black on the tiles, staining the soles of your shoes, as you followed Lucy silently upstairs.

And you try not to remember how on another day it was the same stillness, creation-new. And how Lucy's face had turned, in the moments after you cut open your mother's hand. Pillow blood, sheet blood. Cousin Lucy very still as Maud woke shrieking and grasping.

And you had slept on your anger and it had sprouted into rage, into hatred of every calm hazy morning.

And the weather of the day you were leaving, how it was damp and fumy, and there Lucy was again. All white in the face, and something in there you didn't acknowledge. In you as well. That cut coal-hot and bloody into your very self.

The row of the Brownes watching from the window as you pedalled off on your bike through the elms and up the flagstone path to wherever, away, fuck you, posing fuckers, they couldn't stop you, and they didn't try.

11

Sarah had missed the name of the city, or the town. It was the fifth or sixth stop. One run-down area of the country bled into another. Was she in the South yet? Plants here wanted to grow through concrete, cracked it apart with their long fingers. The sun too had split the earth to help draw the flimsy weeds up tall. Glass shone painfully bright in the windows of the bus station as the Greyhound drew in.

The bus shuddered and was still. The passengers squeezed themselves out onto the pavement to find this was a place of wicked heat. Sarah shivered, took off her hoodie. She felt like tying it around her head so she wouldn't have to feel the omnipresence against her scalp. But once inside the station, which was long and low, she was cold again. Sarah pulled the hoodie back on.

A queue of new boarders were already waiting at the door, watching their bags being thrown into the belly of the coach. An older man reached after his grown son to say, don't be gone long. His manner was jaunty. Short-sleeved shirt cheap but impeccably pressed. Sarah was at her age beginning to marvel at these things. A woman all in white and beige, carrying a lifetime polybag with a pink flower motif, swayed by muttering about the passage of time. Schedules of declining hours, of vague, black-mark deadlines. There was a sort of smut of stress on some people, not on others.

She moved between the press of them, further into the room, though she didn't know why. This place held nothing but wasted time. Sarah looked at her ticket for the list of stops. This to reassure that she was not lost in a recursive misery loop. They had been belting the width of Tennessee, it never seemed to end. The ticket had a slip attached which said 'Not Good For Travel.'

She needed to wash her face. The ladies was clean, a white space and wide. Only a single stall closed. Sarah went to the sink. Her eyes were frightful. And around them rimmed pink like she'd taken the eyeballs out for sleep and had to stuff them back in. She cleaned her face and neck with wetted paper towels. There was a flush, and a woman with her mouth weighed down at the corners came into view in the mirror. Waddled, though she wasn't overweight, not really.

'Hey,' the woman said loudly, coming closer, 'hey, you got some money?'

'Sorry?'

This person in front of her: mortuary skin and eyes very hard and dull. No eyebrows. Hair just sort of there, wisps of dead-yellow.

'I need money. My boys. They ain't et. They need dinner.'

Her breath. Her tee-shirt, old and grey, hung off her body. It said, Southern California Sunshine, 1978, though it probably wasn't that old.

'I'm sorry, but I don't have much with me,' said Sarah, smiling a little. Probably a mistake. Sarah churning inside.

The woman opened her heavy mouth again. 'Well, what you going to do? You better hand me what you got. My boys ain't et.'

'Okay, honey,' doing her American voice, Sarah made a show of taking out her wallet and looking in it. 'I have five dollars. You know, I'm not working right now. I don't have an income, at the moment.' Sarah's little ironic grimace to herself. Sarah's food money fisted, disappearing into the woman's back pocket.

'Five dollars won't feed um. You want us to starve huh?' The woman knocked the emptied wallet to the ground. Sarah crouched to pick it up, kept her eyes locked on the woman. Looming figure. Mouth still open. Angry and breathing in thick snorts.

Sarah was staring, forgetting to smile.

The woman narrowed her little eyes.

Pulled her head back and spat, hard. Then waddled out the door.

The door was still swinging, and Sarah looked at her face in the mirror. She turned on the tap and bent to rub the spit off her cheek. The woman might come back, with a brick from the empty lot to smash at her face and stave it in.

The door swung harder and someone was coming. Sarah folded the corners of herself in. The sink was very cold and clean. The little blue bar of soap milled by age into ridges. It was a policewoman. Sarah hesitated.

The officer looked at her, and then away.

Sarah washed her face again white in her head, dizzy. Sarah splashed water all down her front. Sarah gathered up her things and left. Out in the low open she kept her head down, walked tightly back to the bus to wait in its shadow for departure.

What she would spend her money on

She would use the inheritance to buy back the field with the stone barrow in it. A Neolithic chamber set in the high pasture, which her mother said had kept the venerable bones of Brownes since the time of bronze swords. She would buy it and crack it open like a bottle top, churn the grass around, and there would be planted inside a stone dance of stone men. Some women too with their Boudicca-red waist-length hair preserved against their bodies. She would peel them out like pilchards and dry them under the sun. She would sit by them, witness. And when they had all dried out, she would smash them with a hammer. And sift, remove from them their plate and gold torcs, wooden games, whatever. Their skulls for her table, their bones for a chandelier. And the field left to grow fallow over hard ruts made by her machinery, and any stone shards left to disappear in the muddy water therein.

12

She sipped water, broke the spine of her new book.

It was a two dollar advance reading copy, uncorrected proof, picked up from a rack outside the Strand. A bookshop she had hated because it was a New York institution, and felt like the staff shifted product and spent their carefully poised energy looking down at her. There were no blurbs on the back of this book and, a mercy, the cover lacked the 'a novel' tag after the title, *Show of Passion*. She had bought it for these reasons, and that it was two dollars.

Broadway, 1950s. John was a moderately successful actor. He was neither in the lead role, nor the understudy – the writer was trying not to be coarse, she supposed. John was in love with the director's new wife Kathleen. The director was dying of debt and something else faintly alluded to, involving the liquefaction of his organs, Sarah liked to think, though it seemed to be his kidneys. That was the set up, and the rest of the story would be an easy flat plain with bricks and glass and weeds waving in the distance.

The director was supposed to be unlikeable. Striving towards mediocrity. Gutter mouth, bristly moustache above lips that often drew back in disgust. Sarah smoothed the cover, wondering who lived anyway like John and Kathleen. The two passionate and beautiful, callously unflinching leads of their love story. She wondered if these pretty, papery-thin people had ever woken up at night shaking with lust and with nobody to give that to. Feeling pathetic and so eating apple purée out of the jar, looking out at the street or the screen, because that was sweeter and sharper than the useless gumming sexual throb.

There was a point where it rained both in the story and against the windows of the bus, and Sarah was touched. And wanted to stroke the director's hand as he walked alone through 1950s Times Square, desperately afraid and angry, and to tell him, it gets better, love. I know it will. You can say that to anyone and it will or will not be true. But they won't be able to catch you by the time it isn't.

The pattern on the back of the chair in front came into focus – it was a repeated silver dog in flight, badly rendered in mechanical stitches against the navy backdrop. But each was going somewhere. Even those suspended upside down still depicted gangly legs outstretched, threshing forwards.

Look at the director, cruel with the leading man. How arrogant he is, the author is saying, thinking he knows best, knows art. Director, you won't ever get to see this book through, and a small part of your non-being is aware of this. All fictions are aware of their fictionality. Their twenty-six letters of personhood.

Sarah imagined speaking with the director. In a diner, because diners are where you go to be aesthetically heartbroken. They sat at the counter and twisted their coffee cups a while in silence.

What is it like to be betrayed by your own mediocrity, she started with.

Everything I do declines towards failure, answered the director. He had a fedora on, his father's. He took it off and put it next to a plate of – whatever they ate then. Liverwurst sandwiches. He should say, my wife doesn't understand me. But of course she doesn't, Sarah thought. And there the wife is, walking the dark rainy street with John, right by where she and the director are sitting. A luminescence burns the rain from them both.

Would you look at that whore, said the director.

Now, come on, that's a bit strained, Sarah said. Kathleen the wife. Kennedy the wife. Sarah shook her head. Sirens in the distance for melancholy effect.

Yeah, I guess. I hoped for better, is all, the director said, wiping his eyes. No tears; sweat. I was always there for her, you know? That's what no one ever sees. I was there emotionally,

emotionally and physically. I listened, really.

You didn't stand there with your dick in your hand then?

No, I mean, do I look like a fucking shmuck? Sometimes we fought, especially over interpretation. She said I loved the characters she played, and not her. Jeez. I mean, the cliché of it was just unbearable. He got out a monogrammed handkerchief to wipe off the sweat.

He sounded a bit like Jimmy Stewart, all worked up.

He paused. Played with the bristles of his moustache. It was quite a fine moustache, when you saw it up close. Otherwise, he was hunched and somewhat faceless. He picked up his sandwich and bit in. What colour was liverwurst, even. Milky grey.

That whole impotence line Kathleen used on you back on page forty, that really was too cheap, Sarah said.

A light blinked on in the bus carriage. Perhaps they were stopping or it was merely getting dark.

Is that my signal to go, said the director. Said flatly, but there was neediness at the back of it.

Well, we could go and hover at the window of their hotel room, watch them fuck, scratch a little at the glass, but I think we'd both rather not, said Sarah.

She laid her head on the seatback where the antimacassar should have been and with a little sorrow tucked her book away.

Oklahoma out of all its emptiness had produced a city and the bus was carting through it, late at night or already morning, towards a stop. There was an ache in Sarah's unused legs. In her mind a dull need for something, movement, air, something.

The coach station was decked in old fashioned white and blue tile, with fine signage:

B U S   S T A T I O N   Play it long and elegantly. Skirting the edge of redundancy all the way back around to significance. The interior visible through the glass doorway was also tiled, painted the colour of nicotine residue or the piss of a thirsty man.

Sarah eyed the sad, agentless cargo of the bus stop: the halt, the sick. The lone parent or grandparent transporting their kin cross-country – mobile clamped to their ear, murmuring, 'nuh-huh, yeah it's going alright, no, little shit cried all the way, all the way, but I got her changed now, yeah she shut up,' balancing a baby on their lap at the same time reaching out to swat a second errant child away from a dwindling food supply. Sarah was drawing one, finding in glances of the pen all that sagging sorrow.

Sarah drew a crown on the top of their head, for Liberty.

Since passing over the lounging, flooded Mississippi, Sarah had eaten only chocolates and puffed corn shapes. And not the good kind with jalapeño. Neon orange fake cheese powdered on her lap. She was a thing that consumed, was transported, a crunching cow of the sleepless-and-spat-upon, desecrated variety.

Fuck this. Sarah put away the drawing pad. She was weary. The endless faces she'd seen, most a combination of the anxious, the tired, the strange. There was that couple standing by a payphone. The boy in a black, wet-look jacket with the big-headed skeleton character from *The Nightmare Before Christmas* on it. The girl not overly pretty, a little pasty all over. Both watching the door. He picked up the phone as if to make a call. Replaced the receiver precisely. In their station a kind of vigil.

A police officer came in. Walked the way of American cops, all shoulders, hips, the sausage casing of uniform. He spoke with the driver. Hands locked to his belt. Then they disappeared into the coach. Drugs? She didn't have any. They came back into the station, and suddenly everyone was watching as the cop carried a long rifle, partly wrapped in a towel, holding it aloft like the leg bone of a saint.

The cop with his teeth gritted. Fear passed through the crowd in a wave. Felt almost like nausea, in the walls of the small intestine. Another two officers had appeared.

They walked to the couple by the phone.

It didn't happen in close-up. As if nothing at all had happened, the pair were slinked in handcuffs. The cartoon jacket man was walked in front. He flicked his head to toss a lank of hair from his eye. His mouth uncertain. The woman blotching under everyone's gaze.

The payphone began ringing. The woman started sobbing. A kind of cry near sexual in nature. Then they were gone.

The phone rang out, hollow and metallic.

Sarah sneaked out the back door into the dry of the night.

She walked on every paving stone. Her shoes clopped hollow. She rubbed her arm. Rubbed the creases out of it but not the goosebumps. Fucking Americans and their fucking second amendment, their death-makers packed next to their cocks, or under their beds like monsters.

Turning the corner of the block, Sarah faced an advert in the window of a building under construction: photographs of smiling people. Crisp white collars clean enough to eat, and all of the figures cut up like a children's puzzle. They were imaginary office workers for jobs she felt sure would not exist when the building was finished. If. Above them rose the foetal sttructure, eyeless, rusty girders, nerve endings exposed.

On the ground, a bottle had been broken into the tiniest pieces, a little beach of glitter. Next to it, the greyish screw of a hand-rolled cigarette, the only litter on the street. Oklahoma City. This, Sarah remembered, was the town that had been bombed. But she couldn't remember more, and in any case, felt that to look, to ruminate on it, was to claim. Everyone claims bombings these days, even old ones. I found this pain, it's mine. You, your experience, can't overshadow my pain.

She went back into the station, a little uneasy though there was nothing to be done but to sit on the peeled-paint wire bench. She hugged her body. How many of these shaken travellers would get home tonight, and what was home for them? Scenes like living inside a Hopper painting. Like a failing stage play in which you are a last minute stand-in, no lines. The director gone, dead of his liquefied kidneys, his liverwurst sandwiches. Her head was full of loose change.

The bus was loading again, the smokers stubbed out on the tiled wall and let the butts fall wherever. The yellow eye of the bus station interior retreating. The premise and thickness of a gun. Unstable metaphors. The endless shuddering motion through space.

14

Late Night Piss Poor Diagram of the Artist

Construct in your head a pattern broken up like the inner toss of a kaleidoscope as you wait out night as the man spilling out of the seat next to yours huffs low into his phone to a girlfriend not quite breaking above an angry whisper. Hold yourself far back. Put yourself in one place or in all places in febrile irritated hush. You recite a broken spreadsheet a table made up of single shards of where you've been:

America	England	Cornwall
- Lived in	- Lived in	- Lived in
- Founded but not until late on	- Invaded (lots) (good?)	- Pressed into the toe of itself, is both England and England's sock
- Presidents (45?)	- Monarchs, Londoners	- Family, and other children
- Very grand	- Very garden	- Very cliff
- Hopeful monsters	- Dapper soldiers	- Tin miners
- Drone incendiary	- Brutes with flags	- Shrug

And then art

American Art	English art my love	Cornish art
- Is like Rockwell	- I think of you safely	- Paintings on café walls turquoise sea
- But Marina Abramovic counts	- Tracey Emin though I hate gen x but her, ok	- People on the beach in St Ives. Sandcastles. Dabs. Mother
- I have time To learn Not to fail	- Francis Bacon to name A paltry two and there You failed	- Mum painted Comfort cottage confine and anger Where you failed before

So that was it, Cornwall was mother bad cheap art and England – London – was real art people paid for out of taste and she never questioned what taste was, and America she still had no bloody clue about. Bad émigré, look at yourself. Bad artist, anyway when was the last time you put anything together. And how can you possibly hope to be American if you don't know the American artists. How could I possibly be an artist with my mother alive and dead? How could I possibly want to be American? See that's your problem. Bad daughter. Bad émigré.

She picked up *Show of Passion* and flicked to the point where she had left off.

The moon, shaped like a silver hook, had disappeared many hours before. Leaving in the western sky grades of velvet blue, a slow clasp shutting her in. The bus lights were off but for here and there the screen of a phone, an overhead glow. A dull rumble from the engine swamped her.

The air clammy, cold, smelling of old food and all those crowded bodies, but mostly of the over-used toilet in the back. Sarah cupped her hand to her nose. Wished for a peppermint oil-laced handkerchief. An orange to peel. Inhaling a salty breeze from the sea. There was nothing to do but to breathe through her mouth until the next town.

Outside more of the flat empty earth of Oklahoma, pocked by islands of light – floating farmhouses and spindly, tower-like structures she presumed were for oil. Perhaps Oklahoma rested over a slick black sea. Sarah tapped her fingers on the glass. Beyond, the night was empty, it was unhooked. If she held her breath from this town to the next, would she pass out?

An image of the bus seats imprinted on the blackening landscape.

Another farmhouse. A home glimpsed through the windows, lit up and gone.

An explosion of bright black spots from the dazzling break between the hills.

She opened her eyes when the bus made a swing across the black plain towards a sudden city of lights, which drew nearer and more terrible. The bus pulled into a vast empty lot. Elk City. There was no centre here, no city nor any people. An intersection of strip mall and highway, and the night past the reaches of the streetlamps looking like nights would be in dead cities engulfed in sudden ashfall. The coach steps led off onto the concrete that swayed because she did, ever so slightly. Catkin girl. Paper doll woman.

Four hours into the third day. The petrol station shop was blinding and smelled of doughnuts and bleach. Sarah took money out an ATM and walked the aisles, looking at every sandwich, every can of energy drink. Finally choosing a thin stick of jerky meat plus cheez flavouring, a juice that was too expensive and that was green for health. At the till the change rolled out automatically into a special dish for her collection; a marvel. No hands touched.

Sentimental moments always claw their way in. You need no smell to bring them close, perhaps just a shadow, or nothing; your brain dredges in the mud and there it is:

No hands touched.

Maud had died in the evening. Cousin Lucy had told her, when Sarah had called. The sounds of geese going by. Wrong time of year, but there you are. The hands on the counterpane so delicate and veined, and with nothing to hold. These sorts of harmful details. Why didn't Cousin Lucy hold the hand? Or Aunt Selene?

Sarah's father, Ethan Hamasaki, great love of her mother's life, had not been present. Ethan Hamasaki had had to maintain a pre-measured extra-marital distance, set times for his appearances. The act of his mistress, the mother of his child, finally actually dying was not something he felt the need to see. Maud would have wanted him there. The tips of their fingers curving as he put her hand into his. That white spurt of a scar caressed with a thumb. Even the migrant geese knew that. Maud would have wanted him.

Sarah went outside and watched a large man in a tartan shirt carrying a handful of mustarded hotdogs and a folded but obvious porn magazine up to his eighteen-wheeler.

Sarah leant against the wall. It was warm. The ground and air were sweetly blurred. Smell of fertile earth, drifting from a distant field, invisible somewhere over the great concrete sea. She was trying to think of a poem her mother liked and would recite.

The moon was a ghostly galleon
The moon was a ribbon. The road a ribbon? Of moonlight.
Moorland, blue or black. Purple. The highwayman came riding, riding—

The trucker had got up the steps and now sat behind the wheel, and set the engine idling. He took off his cap. He must have placed the items somewhere because his freed hands were at his eyes. Pressed hard in the sockets. Elbows jabbed out. It took her a little while to realise he was sobbing. The man began hitting at the wheel and the top of the dashboard with fat, mustardy palms.

Perhaps something on the radio.

Perhaps the hotdogs were too bland. Or the porno.

Keep it light.

Sarah walked back from the convenience mart to the bus, stopping to watch a stray dog pitter across the forecourt, then to hand feed it a piece of the cheez jerky. Its snapping chew, dumb, unwavering stare.

On the bus she sat back in her seat, tightened her blanket. The driver had turned the air conditioning up to full blast. She thought of the bus like a Titanic, sailing towards a cold and glinting disaster. The moon is a ghostly galleon, there is no moon in the sky, the new moon is a sunken ship. Her fingers under the blanket gripped her tucked up legs for the little bit of warmth. She stared at her reflection, and dimly beyond it, a giant, dog-eyed country.

What she would spend her money on

She would build a house out of dogteeth, she would build a garden out of food, out of that hard sweet stuff made to look like cigarettes or chalk, lickable cloisters and a sunroom of sugar glass in which she would eat only savouries, and the sound of birds would be the only noise. Silence was a need, pristine was a need. She would buy herself a new self, she would be a girl in blue with narrow wrists fashioned with copper insets. The reassuring heaviness as she rested them in her lap.

17

SANTA FE NEW MEXICO. Sarah was in an anonymous motel room, seated at the small formica table, eating a fast food salad. This scene of perfection lit by an urban dusk and a small table lamp by her bed. She dug about in her food looking for edible cubes of yellow or pink. On the TV John C. Reilly was playing a vampire at the circus. Sarah said aloud, 'this salad is fucking delicious. Pass the vino, darling.' And waved her spork a little, for emphasis. The line familiar. From another film, perhaps. Toasting herself, she necked water from her canteen.

After dinner Sarah lay on the bed toying with her hair.

Thinking of how the motel had bullet-proof glass in the reception and its own security detail, a blunt white car going round and round on the concrete like a hungry shark. The receptionist had mistaken her for a prostitute for no more than a moment or two. That shift in tone. That pinch of courtesy thrown in at the end with the keys.

Sarah had gone up to her room and shed sour clothes. Then the shower, oh God. Moaning and scrubbing furiously. The water running down her, carrying the skin oils and crumbs and bus residue down the drain. Till it ran clear at last. That shower into which she could go again, right now, if she felt the urge.

She closed her eyes, shifting her bare legs against the lumpy cotton quilt. The bed was not uncomfortable, and the lamp light gentle. In fact it was wonderful; it was the most comfortable place she could wish for.

The sound from the movie scratched at her. She changed the channel.

The news was on the slow end to a war. Telling it in a rueful tone. America hadn't won, hadn't lost, didn't know what it had done. Footage of children, wrapped in beautiful but dusty clothes. Carefully isolated images of people going about their lives. The voiceover turned upbeat.

The next story about a lottery.

The next story about a dog that rescued three children from a fire.

Sarah could not sleep so she got up and left the TV burbling to itself. Headed downstairs in her nightdress and slip-on shoes, clutching a plastic bucket from her room.

In motels there is a little over-lit enclave open to the elements, housing an ice machine. You can visit it any time, and when you have nothing to do is a good time to do so. Ice for the possibility you've brought champagne to your motel room. Ice as a palliative for the ills of the night. She pressed a button and listened to the clank as the bucket filled. It was warm here, the air luscious as it should not be beside a motel car park. The ice bubbled against her fingers and wrist. She put a cube up to her mouth and pressed it there. Luxury. The lights of the security car swept across the pavement. Sarah thought of stepping out, standing there until the guard came round again. Just to give him a look.

Someone was playing music with a hypnotic low bass. A man called to another, 'Jay, where'd you go, man?' It was amiable, soft. Sarah went up the concrete steps. She passed Jay pulling himself up the blue banister, calling back to his friend.

'Am here,' he said.

It was the night, it was yearning and waiting and passing through. She ate a piece of the ice, sucked on it, crunched it, back to her room. She ate half the ice bucket, melted the rest with the heat of her body, against her neck, between her thighs, trying to cool something incapable of being cooled inside her.

18

Somewhere between motel dreams and motel TV you can follow the war and its fading importance by the voice of the newscaster. You need not listen, just mind the range of how far up and down, or split and hesitant it runs. In Helmand Province today one American soldier was killed and seven others wounded in a bomb blast – listen to the calm enunciation, and you can hear that the road was potholed and the country poor. Overhead, black planes with no riders. No one takes true ownership of those. No one draws art on their sleek flanks.

In the voice of the reader, dry and dusty, you hear the segue into now to our field correspondent: and there is the blackness of a night strafe behind him, a discord of lights and muffled crashes. The correspondent reports from there only because the number is a significant milestone in American dead.

Behind the correspondent it's all being toppled. Every stone and every child you cannot see. Every man in a militarised zone counts as a combatant, once he's dead.

In firm, teacherly tones, the correspondent reminds you of your obligation to a western world. To follow the narrative. The narrative of a book that is so often just the word death death death in the footnote. In the modern world the footnote is where less diversion and more humanity is to be found crouching, trying to be true in the least possible space.

What do you do with your brush? You make soothing shapes to forget your complicity. Or you stop. There has been no poetry since the holocaust. Not true. There has been no honest art without a footnote to all the evils we do. Dishonest art is the freest, boldest kind. Sarah could make neither. How to force through in art, try to speak meaningfully, to claim in big letters:

I am here to stop the war!

Citizens!

Of the world! I am here for peace not just to say there has been death!

Sarah lay on her inky hair, face pushed down on the motel pillow in the motel dark and feeling over herself the flash of car headlights outside in New Mexico.

Her pillow, her head, her complicity intersecting at too many points.

19

Sarah opened the window to let the sun in, determining to buy herself a bottle of something. Still lemonade, a sweet acidic wash. She would get to the cabin that night.

She went into the bathroom and drank from the tap. The wall behind the sink was mirrored and in it she looked at herself. The strap of her nightdress had slipped down. The pillow had done strange things to her hair and her eyes were slothful. I'm a slob, she thought. Someone should draw me, every descending thread of hair, and make me – just make me.

Outside she hung back in the shade watching the security car and the man inside it looking solemn and then spaced out. He scratched the tip of his nose, adjusted his polarised glasses. Perhaps he had broken up a fight last night, or yanked a client away from the woman, the boy, the body he had paid for with a wodge of notes. Behind those glasses were the eyes of a stranded man.

Sarah wished she had that kind of reflective shield; she struck a pose instead. Hands low on her hips like she owned herself. This was the American desert and she had begun again, okay. No one cared where or who she was and the sky was a precise, unwavering blue.

20

The Valle Grande is northwest of Santa Fe.

A powder-grey car struck out across the parched land. Stones sprinkled on the light sandy earth, around the evergreen bushes. Mesas rose like scalloped jelly moulds filled with strata: white, yellow, red. Sarah drove; the car swept an arc across a foreign land, home.

A town in the distance, stacked boxes all of adobe.

A sign that indicated Native American lands, but the name of the tribe only half-caught and in any case wouldn't have been known.

An hour. An inch of the sun. Then there was something on the road ahead, a small brown sign which glinted. Sarah frog-kicked the brakes.

RIO GRANDE SCENIC OVERLOOK

She turned in and parked. There was roadkill on the next parking spot. Stuck gravy of broken mammal on a hot blacktop. An animal stupid enough to die by reversing car is a piteous thing. Beyond it, the land gave the impression of falling away.

She walked over to the edge and looked down: dead gold grass tumbling, and sandy rocks, bushes, tiny cactuses. And there against frugal aridity was the great river in dusky green with trees at the banks. Not so very wide but sinuous and in good lungs – roaring forty feet below. Sarah felt like it would be glorious to dip into the green wetness, to drink gulps of the microbe-rich water as if it were a wheatgrass drink. Or to ride it feet first, screaming. Things she did not have a fear of: heights, drowning. But there was no path down and the way would be too steep. Snapknee.

Sarah from where she was could see the river flowing north to south and how it took the trees with it. Rose up onto the plain and swivelled and slaked, and was not, she thought, the

East River or the Thames. Nor any river made for boats and grey commerce. The sun did not glitter on the green river's surface but beamed through the water itself so that it shone.

Sarah tried to sit on the bonnet of the car, but jumped at the metal burn against her thighs. She sat instead on the dusty ground and leaned into the sun as long as she could bear it, with the inner sides of her arms and wrists exposed. Then took out her drawing pad and did what she could. A single unbroken line for the geometry of mesa, river edge, scrub. Afterwards she drove off and followed for some time the strong and lively river as faithfully as possible.

What she would spend her money on

She would get huge slabs of carcass from best-beloved cattle. Smooth marbled flesh. She would hang these in a specially prepared cellar and frighten herself with their bodies and pungency in the dark. She would buy up old china tea sets, the kind so thin, translucent, they seemed unwell and she feared to hold them. She would return to candle light and drink beef broth to stave all fevers. She would choose to be that kind of aristocrat, to live the austerities of another age. She would keep a collection of artisan knives and cut the cattle flesh for hanging on an antique clockwork roaster that would dangle and twist the carcass part over the flame. She would watch the carcass become meat as it cooked in the huge yellow-tiled kitchen. To her dry lips apply a balm of suet. She would eat handfuls of the cooled and bloody meat, in the salon all alone with the window letting in humid air off the creek. Vases of lilies on coffee tables, too high to see if she had guests.

The day was long and hers alone. American lonesome. She stopped at turnoffs, at petrol stations, at viewpoints. She drank juice, she sang to the dashboard. The afternoon yawned and stretched. The landscape altered by degrees that seemed miniscule until they seemed radical. Sarah and car crawled up along a ridge with low trees below in gulches, and then only pine, and a darkness of it closing in like a pelt, the road dustier. Higher she drove, through passes carved out of pocked sandstone and grey tuff. The sky clarified, in aspect an almost winter sunniness. Sarah drove onwards through states of wonder and into the mountains and dark, real forests that she had viewed in satellite imagery once in her room in New York all fallen away.

The sunset, the sunset blinding, the sunset grading away, and these divisions left behind.

Sarah came into the caldera with the dark. She lipped along the Valle Grande road. A dim shape on the distant side: her cabin. The sensor light clinked on, tracing the eaves and the shale roof, the flank of the rough wooden wall. The smell of pine bark came red astringent through the car window. Untempered land, and her heart bursting momentarily in the way of those things.

From her bed under the low sloping roof Sarah could hear the wind shaking the dark and unmet forest. If wind had mouths to blow through, life would be far more disturbing. This wind was needy, hollow. As if it had had some human lover once on a summer night many years since, who was now dead.

Sarah sat up and leant forward. Banged her head lightly against a beam and fell back. She pouted as she rubbed her head. Little gasp, as if for an audience. She groped on the floor for her pad and dip pen. Clicked on the lamp and wrote in burnt sienna India ink a footnote on the last picture in her pad (the picture of the Rio Grande, streaks of imagined spilt green against pale dirt):

'Wind, I am alone you are alone we are the push of particles heated and cooled.'

The ink speckled and Sarah blew on the page. Silence, wind. The floors of the cabin creaked below her. The little red Scandinavian curtain closed tight.

She looked at five pages of her sketchbook she had filled with drawings of a small branch. She had found it, a twisted thing, on the doorstep shedding black flakes. The red wood flesh visible under minor splits in the bark. This is good, the split, the slake of ink beneath a brush.

Outside it was getting light. Trees, juniper, ponderosa, spruce perhaps, waded away into the long grass towards the dense collective that covered the hill. From one of the trees had come the branch. You could feel in the presence of forests an imposition.

But for that moment Sarah was sweet and raw. She pulled the blanket over her shoulders. First nights are like this in an unacquainted place, like being with a new lover. The scent of the room. Going to sleep unsure. Waking up unsure.

Heightening and furzing at her stability of self. It takes time to fill the drawers with letters, staplers, with buttons and USB cords of unknown provenance. To get herself, jaw and fingernails, firmly embedded in the space.

Sarah thought a moment, and then tore off the corner of the picture, the part she had written on. She curled her pretty pink lip. Sentimental. Spirit of the land rubbish. Touch the stones and ground the body, whatever. She was here for reinvention, and she was here to be self-sufficient and to get over those sorts of stupidities. She saw her hand against the pinewood windowsill and felt tiny and without friends. She still felt the sway of the Greyhound. How many days does a transformation take, and how must she defend against her own softness until then.

23

A body in an empty bed, a body sullen in an occupied bed, both parallel a body in a grave.

London. Above the phone repair shop, up a stairway with no natural light, into a space with four others, each one a personality she had to pretend not to care about. With the door open she'd made conversation, with it shut she had stared in silence at the plaster-swirled ceiling, failing at art.

'Sarah.'

That boy, the actor, skinny jeans, every bone of note on show.

Sarah at the window smoking so she could have a prop. Yor was sprawled on bedsheets. Showing off his hip bones. Flecks of hairs on his chest as he ran a hand through them. A delicate disarrangement of blankets. Doe eyes.

'It's the fucking cold,' Sarah had said, oblivious, 'it's fucking – the damp in here. I can't put the heating on, so I just sit under this rank duvet, feeling hungry.'

'Sarah, I don't want to talk about this now.'

'Why not, Yor?'

'Don't call me "Yor" for God's sake. You call me Yor to your friends. I hate it. I told you, it's obnoxious, yeah?'

'Yorick. Yorick.' She could still feel how tender his belly skin was when she prodded it.

A sigh, a twenty-three-year-old boy's sigh: 'He hath/borne me on his back a thousand times; and now, how/abhorred in my imagination it is! my gorge rims at/it. Here hung those lips that I have kissed I know not how oft—'

He had never been any good. But then, neither had she, back then. They both were too much concerned with the displacement of the moment. And their hair. She at being blunt and insular and him all scruffy and delicate. Sarah had thought: let's blow this room to fucking smithereens. Now she thought, poor children. You sort of loved each other, a tiny crumb of hope for yourselves, and what did you let happen?

Yor coming up behind her, gently. Skeletal cheekbones. Sarah had once spoken too much. Below the window, the street. And a writer had already said of London that there was a man with an ugly jacket trying to sell watches when he should be in Camden, and in any other season but this.

'Mmm. You could kiss me,' Sarah had said, 'but you'd better not. I am a creature of blanket: I am art with my hands and a set of eyes, and feet that are always numb with the cold. Heat is when atoms move, isn't it. Vibrate. Cold is when everything fucking stops. Time stops. Light becomes a lump of solid flesh.'

Your late teens and early twenties as a time of performance art watched by hardly anyone at all. But you think everyone.

'Well, anyway,' Yorick had said, flopping back down on the bed, 'Sarah. I don't know. Fucking, move in with me then. My place is warmer. You'd get to have me to yourself all the time. It's actually in Shoreditch too?'

'Yor, why is that last part a question and the first part an order? Never mind. I don't care. I have to get ready soon, my cousin is in town. She wants to talk.' Her lips thin in a wry smile, turning her head just so. She made herself into a perfume advert in a dank flatshare.

Electricity at his place had been cut off due to non-payment. Blackout conditions, Londoners thrive. Candle sex and smoking joints to eighties music, skins and skin, snickering. And it had been either that week or the week after they'd moved in together, and half a year later, they'd just about been broken up, when he died, freak stroke in the toilets of some club. He'd been borderline disordered in his eating or maybe it was coke that did it. Had she actually called him Yor in real life? What had his real name been? In the dark nothing came to her. Anyway. The bodies we've been and had peel away. All these spindly skeletons, small as a flicker in our heads. Would any of them remember her, at the instance of her remembering them? The line is, your last death is when the final person utters your name aloud. Too bloody cruel. Maybe he had family still talking of him.

Maybe he heard her now.

'Yor,' she said, then after a moment – 'Sebastian, ah.'

24

The massive windows at the front of the cabin faced the prairie. Sarah went out the back door onto a little bit of decking, down three clattering steps into the long grass. It was still morning. Flanking the house, the dark wood fur of the mountains was still in shade. To the left, a set of overgrown ruts, an old access road perhaps, headed towards the trees like a blues song trailing off.

Sarah walked out to the right, over the plain until the cabin shrank to a doll's house. She stood and listened. Insect klitter and vuuv. New York had always talked over her, but here, this land hushed. There was the feeling of coolness against the skin of her arms. Across the impossibly wide field, a herd of animals grazed, on the move perhaps. Her eyes followed a wave rushing through the grass. From the far right side of the valley, shimmering it ran. Ran by her, kept running. Eddied the grass against the homestead, and was off again beyond it, maybe fifty metres until it dropped, long before the cessation of grass.

Little splinters of thought. No one knew where she was. Air in, and out. Maud had stepped through this great meadow with nothing to hold onto. A fast, little Cornish woman in a linen dress. But was it a Maud young and healthy, with her silver-fox lover, or Maud in recovery, brittle and blasé, or Maud after the estrangement from Sarah, her cold face smiling when it had to – here did not have to. Her empty voice as she spoke into the telephone, 'Sarah, I'm going to be away for a little while and you won't be able to reach me.'

Anyway, Sarah thought as she began to walk back, Maud left me all this. Thick sunlight over her trembling shoulders. The grand valley breathing. Am here, she thought. Some dusky pinkish dab caught her attention: it was a house, on the other side of the Valle, beside the top road. Neighbours. She wondered how anyone could already be living in a place so brilliant. What world was theirs, dim against all of this?

She walked and her cabin grew to human proportions again. She brought order to her thrown hair and leant against the wooden wall, pressing. Hoping she'd get no splinters. Hoping she would. Closed her eyes and let her mouth slip open. Mine, me, mine, here.

Her stomach rumbled, the thunder of a small god.

25

There was one good photo, taken before puberty. Sarah in her mother's lap in her cousin's cast-off woollen jumper and leggings, looking away from the camera, up at her mother. There are no other clues.

Something else: that summer evening they went for a walk and Maud had them stop in a field. It was sunset, and a fence kept them from falling off the cliff into a golden sea.

'Are there horses walking down there?' Sarah had asked.

'Yes,' said Maud, 'down the path there. It's very steep, isn't it?'

'Yes. We don't have any horses?'

'No. It would be cruel.'

'Why would it be cruel?'

'Because horses frighten me,' Maud said.

Sarah nodded. They had long faces, and their teeth were very big.

'If I owned a horse, I feel like I would ride it until it dropped from exhaustion under me,' Maud said.

'Until it fell over from tiredness?' said Sarah.

Maud squinted as the horses walked down the cliff path. Slow, pulling at the tall plants, waving their tails. 'Until it was dead, probably,' she said. 'I wouldn't stop until it had given me everything and taken me far further than it could.'

'If it was a clever horse, it would just stop and not budge if you tried to do that. Did you ever have a horse before, when you were little?'

'No, even way back then we couldn't afford horses. And Granddad knew we'd be cruel to them. We rode bicycles, just like you and Lucy.'

'Millie, in my class, her dad runs the riding school. Her horse is called Chitty.'

'Yes, I know, you've told me before. Don't be tedious. Do you want to go riding?'

A pause.

'No, I'm not the kind of girl who likes horses,' said Sarah. 'I like to watch them walking about, that's all.'

That night she had dreamed of watching horses far away. And of their big empty eyes and mouths that moved around oddly, full of those elderly teeth. There was something about the body of a horse and how it was not her body. And how her mother was warning her without saying it clearly. A horse will carry you on her back until she dies. Or there wasn't anything to it.

And another day, years later: Maud was sitting stiffly on a wicker chair on the autumn lawn. A crackle in the air of almost-frost. Sarah placed a mug of tea by her slippers in the grass. Maud nodded.

'That cherry tree there, in the centre. I hate it.' She said, 'it's all rumpled and diseased. Don't you think the trunk looks like a toad? Squatting there like a fat old ugly toad. We really should do something about it.'

'Hmm,' said Sarah.

'I'm going to—' said Maud. She got to her feet. Thin then, but recovered. Or as far as the doctors could tell. She crossed the lawn to the tool shed. Sarah watched her go. And listened.

The axe bit the wood with a cheerful puck, puck. Sarah pulled her sleeves down over her fingers.

'It's going to take ages, Mum. You should see if you can call a man in to do it.'

'No, don't be ridiculous. It won't take long.'

'Mum. Mum,' Sarah said.

'Shut up, Sarah. Don't you have somewhere else you can be? You can be such a… a…'

Sarah left.

From the library she heard, puck, puck, puck. Three fucking hours of axe bites from Maud's scrawny swinging arms. There was no crash as the tree came down, more of a groan, a shuffle from the high branches as it hit and sank through the tool shed roof.

Maud in the kitchen, pallid and sweaty, drinking water.

'There, that's better. You didn't think I could do it. Never underestimate an artist. I'd have torn it out with my nails if the axe hadn't worked.'

Maud had never painted horses. Perhaps there was something to that, which made her more vulnerable. Some terrible thing in her past that must always and ever be fought. Whatever. Who even has the energy.

Last bit: Maud in the wheelchair, Sarah pushing her out of the hospital. Reading a book about Frida Kahlo. Selene had brought her a shawl from the attic: silk, red, and intricately patterned. Maud picked at the tassels as she read choice extracts to Sarah. The two of them rattling about like dried peas on the near-empty bus to St Mawes. Maud still reading aloud, though one old biddy in a mint mac at the front kept turning round to stare. Sarah, for once not embarrassed, scowled right back.

Welcome to Esta. Elevation 4,460ft.

Esta. This place. Twenty or so miles to the northeast of the Valle Grande and into the Sangre de Cristo range of the Southern Rockies. The iconography and naming she could ponder. Sarah behind the wheel, neat in denim jeans and blood red jumper, touching her collar bones. Names are little containers and you could say that all mountains demand sacrifice, give of their grandeur, so well done there. But what the hell were the conquistadors trying to say about Esta? What do you contain with 'this place'.

But the town itself was unexpectedly endearing on first glance, a kitschy hybrid of wild west and ski-town styles, with log-fronted saloons guarded by chainsaw-cut wooden bears and half a dozen motels made to look like chalets, all advertising vacancies. Low season since there was no snow, and almost no one about.

Driving down Main Street led her to a grey, washed-out building that housed a non-chain supermarket. Sarah got out, wobbled, and checked around. The air felt just as clean as in the valley. The sun circled overhead as if there was nothing between her skin and its rays but a few billion molecules of space. But beyond the market lands, a pile of tires and rotting cars in the bleached grass. With perfect timing a dog barked twice. Tugging a muscle in Sarah's chest. From some movie, she thought, standing on the edge of the town. *Stand By Me.* It's always from some movie, or book, or TV show.

Cold air blasted through the automatic doors.

The tiny fresh produce section contained corn, potatoes white and sweet, some greens, and a stack of strawberry punnets. Fat as infant fists. They'd be hydroponics, nothing of the earth, tasting of strawberry-flavoured saliva.

Sarah made a rotation. Hauled sacks of rice, dried beans, and frozen greens into her basket. Someone had left in the cabin an unopened gallon of olive oil and several containers of salt as if to keep evil from the empty house. So that was kind. Last things she picked out were twelve lemons and a bag of sugar and then made her way to the checkout.

The cashier a girl leisurely popping gum. Scanning in time to the blips.

'So, you here on vacation?'

Sarah looked up. Staring back at her a pair of heavy-lidded, delicately painted eyes, bright blue. A red mouth, breaking open a little.

'Uh, yep,' Sarah said in her American accent.

Bleep, crack. Quick nails, glitter-black, tapping out on the ancient register the code for the lemons. Collect the details while there's time: a high-necked black top clinched the girl's throat. Tiny breasts. Early twenties or early thirties or ageless. That slight smirk. Sloping shoulders and blonde hair slightly lank. Playing the difference between vibrant and languid, the browless model of a Renaissance painter. But something molten in there, shifty.

Sarah scratched at the take-a-penny-leave-a-penny tray, moving a penny around. She still didn't understand how the tray was meant to work.

'I'd guess you're here a month or two, right?' said the cashier. 'Got these pintos, making a few stews. And tampons. I get this soap too. I love the way it smells.' The girl held the box to her nose, and managed not to make that odd. Maybe a bit odd. 'Vanilla… and roses. Blown roses.'

'Taking an interest, hmm?' said Sarah. Her flirtatious voice came from another body. A body not wrenching inside. Someone fashioned of whale bone and cream and tar.

The girl looked her up and down, which was quick. It didn't take much time to get all she needed. Sarah had seen those eyes before. Not just thinking generally. But she didn't have time to place them before the cashier interrupted.

'Maybe, girl. Maybe you're the first interesting person I've seen today.' Bubblegum crack.

'I'm an interesting person, people've told me that.'

The girl smiled again, showing no teeth. 'I never said you were. Yet.'

Sarah shrugged the shopping bags up against her body. Her hair fell across her face. Mouthed behind that hair some strange words that if the cashier had heard – well, she did not show. They both sensed another customer arriving, but didn't turn away. Until Sarah did.

Outside, a line of cars were waiting for a small group of deer to pick their way across the asphalt. Half the does already stood chewing in the ditch by the petrol station. Watching them Sarah thought, maybe the cashier only meant she was interesting because she looked different. She gave a long breath out, rubbed her scalp, pulled out the soap from its box. The label said original scent, it had no right to be more than basic. But to her it had the smell of incense, the odour of cut pine. Fuck was this pointless enchantment.

27

Sarah lurched awake. Her shoes were melting from resting on the iron of the wood stove. The fire, sending the shadow of its fingers into the cracks on the floor, probed the air with tiny sounds. Dark everywhere else, and immensely dark outside. Miles of solitude like an immense lashed navy blue canvas. She pulled the scratchy quilt closer round her.

She at least had cooked. A stew of paprika beans and oiled garlic, not too bad, almost like something a real person would make. Not a ghost from the bus. Wandergeist. And for dessert she'd drunk powdered milk made up in sugar-water with dried mint. It had dimmed her thoughts and she had slept, or half-slept. Pretended to sleep so she could indulge in images of the Warne.

It wasn't that she was weak, she told herself. She had loved and loved still the turn of the door handle on the old greenhouse, the dustbeams in the library where the books made ribbed noises behind their wire cages. Where she had read *Jane Eyre* on a leather stool and wished she had been an orphan. And Jane Eyre with iron gaze had whispered curses back, all variants on ignorant, spite-filled creature.

And now you are all alone, ten years alone. But you didn't get to be young and orphaned, only twenty-seven with nothing earned, nothing brought to life only clever snark and raw footless optimism. Will you pack the inheritance in envelopes, lick them sealed and post off to charity? Will you ever do anything worthwhile? This isn't even your house. You came here and broke in and set a fire. You should be drunk by now on port kept in the dirt-floored basement. You should scrawl your name with your fingernails on the fucking skirting board where no one will see but maybe in another ten years a small boy, and it will frighten him.

Sarah blinked and worked hard to feel nothing. In the hush the floorboards creaked. Fire danced. Keys on the wall, deeds in the bag, money tied up in lawyers' offices. No burdens. This dislocated, lonely body of hers. But what do I do, she thought with rising panic. What terrible thing was she going to do.

In the morning – it will be morning in five hours, not too long – I'll plaster my drawings all over the walls. Sarah pulled the quilt up to her mouth. There, isn't that a plan. Throw open every drawer and finger receipts and file them in the bin. Scrape off all this Maud that was everywhere clamming up the joint. She'd take off her clothes and empty her mind – it would be easy then – lean out the window and yell. Into the green, across the flanks of the volcano. No fucking up or fear or self-effacement. In a new body at last.

She took off her shoes and placed them beyond the light of the fire.

28

How delicate the image you've created of yourself. The imaginary decree that you, yourself, is in any way iron-banded, sustainable, deserving of love. Your mother painted you whenever she needed a little girl to carry bundles of lavender or hold the net above the rock pool. Back when nobody wanted the pictures, she made you wriggle into the old dress and stand on the platform in the little brick studio in the garden. The buds in your chest hurt but Maud kept telling you stand straight for godssake you're wasting my time. You kept focusing on the way Lucy could wrap her pinky round her wrist and you couldn't do that with any of your fingers. Which meant you were a fat mess. And Maud wanted to put you in her pictures so you'd be fat forever. Maybe if you had a friend they'd put a friendship bracelet on your fat wrist and it would be a nice distraction. You watched a house spider building a web where the ceiling met the studio walls, just above your mother's shoulder. A spider is an artist, it beads out its parlour as slowly as a woman marks out her lines of sight on a canvas, patches in a garden and a pudgy girl and a little grey smoke from a chimney, humming to herself.

A little radiator heated the studio, but poorly. The bodyside closest it cooked while the side away from it was left chilled through. You'd shuffle to turn and turn back again, before the painter noticed and rebuked.

It wasn't really you that Mum immortalised in paint. It was that blonde girl, ethereal, fully white-English. Later, Maud would label her 'Little Belle' because it was a name that would work in most markets. You were never more than a prop, a point of reference for Mum's imaginary Little Belle. She who was always little, a dainty smudge of white and yellow and rose and green. No matter how much Sarah changed shape.

Where was it you'd read of the curse that trapped the girl inside the painting? *The Witches*. What a delicious idea, that Little Belle was a lost soul. Silently screaming. Once, you scratched off a little of her, just the hair by her face, with your fingernail. Under that top flake of yellow, black hair. Yours.

You scratched, very carefully, at her eyes. Worked underneath to their real shape, real colour. The dot of her pink mouth next – but with that, you'd obliterated the face. Your undernail ached. A ratch-ratch sound. Back across the frost-bitten grass you had walked, ten years ago, picking at your nailbeds, hoping to find a new thing to claw and this time draw blood.

29

Sarah rapped at the screen door; it seemed frail. About to jump from its hinges and fall against her. She shifted back, tried the doorbell a third time, let out a little cough. The sun plastered her limbs with its heat cleanly. She brushed an insect from her arm. She had walked out across the wilds. Investigating out of boredom, she thought. Sugar. Cup of sugar.

Her neighbour's house was built of adobe, terracotta coloured. Sturdy and ancient-looking. The corners and wooden beams jutted out smoothly from the past. It was on two levels, and stepped. A pyramid structure. She admired the open porch, a pillared, hardwood construction with a sloped roof. Something of it from a TV cowboy series Aunt Selene had flicked over to every Sunday morning. There should've been a tin cup hanging from the pillar near a butt of fresh water but instead there was a twisting wind chime. It made the place seem lonely. Sarah had spotted a terrace above, accessible through the upper-floor windows. People ought to smoke out there at night and count the fixity of the stars—

She turned to see a man, opening the first of the two doors. He was a dark jumble, and then he was leaning easily with his arm against the inside of the screen door. Assessing, silent. He reeked of confidence and that special way of havoc that seems for a moment a good idea.

'Hello,' she said.

'That you down there?' The man nodded his head in the direction of the cabin.

Sarah looked down the hill, at the meadow, the blackness of the cabin against the green of the woods. She nodded and gave a half smile.

'Huh. I heard they were selling it,' he said. 'Or are you renting?'

Sarah told him, 'It's mine, now.' He rocked against his arm. Brown hair heavy at the top, but close cut at the back and lower sides, perhaps to suit or tame the clumsy bent of the curl. An old-fashioned look, the kind that boys in Williamsburg wear, wide-mouthing their mason jars of iced beer.

'Nice hair,' she said.

'Is,' he said, looking down. 'Anyway,' he paused and raised his head, 'name's Theo. Theodore Coronado.'

'Sarah Browne.'

She heard his cleverly broken sentences. He now looked clever, and innocent. She went up and down on her toes. Would he ask her in? It seemed as if he was a World War II naval bomb washed up on a beach. Only maybe unconscious of his capacity.

'The cabin belonged to my mother, Maud Browne. The painter?'

Her English lips, posh, accented words like pressed roses. She stood down, gave herself distance. The paintings. The posters. The mousemats, the coasters. The main thing was to wonder if he despised her yet or soon.

'Yeah, I remember Maud. She came a few summers,' he said. 'Gam helped round her cabin. Collected her too.' He paused and smiled. 'I mean, your mom signed some prints.'

'Gam?'

'She's out right now,' he said, 'seeing friends, I guess.'

'And… are you coming out?' said Sarah. 'It's quite a nice day. Or I could come in?'

'You thirsty?' He smiled and opened the screen door an inch.

The man had stubble that was either unkempt or deliberate. He looked at Sarah steadily through the mesh. This invulnerable playfulness of his. This was all getting a little out of hand. If he licked his lips. They were a little dry. That would be it, she'd start to grin, or sweat.

Theo eased off the post and flicked open the door. Moving forward as if to offer her his hand. Sarah, down on the cropped yard, smiled and recanted the smile, and looked at her feet. All games fall apart if you acknowledge them too directly.

On the second step of the porch, Theo tripped. Fell over his stupid laconic gait. Sarah with a split second to put her arms out to catch him instead stood back. Hands held up. Let him drop. Afterwards she laughed.

'Fuck,' he said after a short delay.

'Are you alright? Is anything broken?'

'Well, I landed on my fucking face.' He pulled himself up to a sitting position with small sharp intakes of breath, and patted imaginary dust off his chin and shoulders. He winced, testing his arm. Now the aura around him had cracked and he looked to be thinking, well shit, as he picked shards of it off like glass.

'I saw you from up there,' he pointed up vaguely to the second floor, 'thought I couldn't just let you stand there looking so neglected—'

'Yes, maybe I looked like I was selling something?' Sarah said. 'I'm pleased you came down, even if you've uglied yourself a bit.'

Theo closed his eyes, tight smile. Maybe he was going to try and laugh it off, but then he didn't. Hobbled to standing. There was room in that smooth, scuffed face for a lot to happen. She would like to tell him he had a grimy cut that was starting to ooze. The buzz she got from being around mild injuries and how it might make her do something odd, like sidle over and press her head against his and lick his wound for him. You forget the taste of blood, and rarely have the chance to be reminded.

'Better come back later,' he said, smiling again. 'I'll patch myself up and introduce you to Gam.'

Sarah nodded. Another person would have offered to help him. Would have cooed over his scrapes, let him lean on her, bandaged his arm with gentle fingers and touched a fresh warm wet cloth to his face. A strange sort of lying, it seemed to her.

Sarah was already walking away with her hands tightly and preventatively folded, before the stranger got himself, limping, out of sight.

Back at the cabin Sarah balanced thoughts like books on the top of her head.

She took a while to think about Theo, to remember the way the sleeves of his tee-shirt circled his arms, that sort of thing. The steady gaze flicker, smile flicker. The way he'd looked after he'd fallen and cut himself. She picked a little of the flaky bark on the cabin wall. The wood remnants on her fingers smelt distinctive, like a scalp. Sarah thought of breathing in the stranger's scent from his hair, pushing her hands up under his shirt, up into the mess of chest hair – she'd press her body against his and the taste in her mouth would be the anticipation of kisses. Her lips twinged. Having not tasted his gritty blood, not having ruined it all beforehand.

She went inside and drank tepid water until her throat relaxed.

Out the kitchen window and beyond her fetishes was, she noticed, the echo-landscape of one of her mother's paintings entitled *Buttercup Lawn*. Without buttercups, but with that kind of unreal scoop of greeny-goldenness. In her mother's later works all that sodden light was everywhere. The dew too wet, and that depthless quality, unbearable Technicolour cottagey blurred flower mushiness.

But beyond all that the forest began, and she noticed a pine slumped into the others, branches crossed and crushed in a way that permitted no even line of beauty. Firewood filled a sagging woodshed to the right of the faded path. There was no stubbled man in plaid chopping logs, leaning just so.

She only wanted to be spared, to continue resisting.

She stepped into a great hot bath sprinkled liberally with salts, and sat there humidifying until all seemed blood-warm and level. Naked and steaming she got out, went to the bedroom dripping still and lay down on the bed. She felt her breathing hot into hotter air and it made her head throb. Her body, throb.

She had been thinking of the cashier for hours indirectly.

A silhouette against the rich folds of a tapestry.

An icon of a body and a certain light on that body and the sweet forceful pressing of girl against her. Sarah's hands inching in her own fur. Couldn't call it anything but that. Cute names, no. She had wet fur and her fingers felt right away for the flesh that mattered. The cat tongue rasp of it. Two-fingered friction. The cashier no-name with the limp hair and the large watery eyes and attitude of celebrity, made for imprecise thoughts. Strawberry tongue. Wild strawberry small and puckered lips.

Into a room without features but somehow sumptuous walks the cashier. The cashier's walk imagined as loose, unaffected. The cashier unbuttoning work clothes with blurry gestures. The clothes puddle over a chair, a huge velvet chair, a huge puffed velvet red chair into which the girl falls, kicking up her legs. Her tiny underwear is pretty pink and rips apart to scraps and her and her. Sarah is blushing all over. She is steaming warm. She is licking at the girl's fur and like a cat's tongue against a human tongue she is fingering herself and pawing the breasts of the cashier and she has more hands than ever, and their bodies push and rock. Sarah's breath. Sarah's breasts, her nipples swollen. How would the girl moan? How would she narrow her eyes and lean backwards, that throat, those little breasts of hers rubbed pinched? Everything brightly coloured to a narrow throbbing strip. She opened her eyes in the dream. And at the threshold of the imagined room without qualities he was there.

Had the girl gone? No. Sarah's fingers circled, studying the lines in her curls. Well, are you here then? He seemed to be. Sarah, bemused. She liked the way men were, their bodies, the difference, murmurously enjoyed the way they tended to do things, but she never, almost never, touched herself thinking of them.

But there he was, in stance the nakedness already highlighted and concealed by a white shirt over his arm. The man vulnerable is a work of art and posed like this. The backdrop was red, was soft, and herself. The cashier got up and brushed by Theo on the way out the door. Sarah was a jealous woman even in her fantasies. Even with her own body.

Theo moved towards her. He bent down on his knees, he pressed his head of dark curls to her chest. Theo held her and his arms were sinuous and his skin warm. Muscles visible on his torso, Sarah could rib them with her thumb like the spines of books though she did not like to touch them though she did. Contradictions are unwelcome in fantasy. She was about to pull away when his hand shot down her body and grabbed her firmly by the fur and his fingers were inside her. And he was looking her directly in the eyes. Flashes of a smile that hinted and. And his tongue at the corner of his lips was a red fold. Was in past her lips. She held her breath. He pulled out his fingers and he pushed his cock in slowly, hard into her and those strange ribbed muscles were against her. Sarah gasping and made use of herself. The vow of her breath. Blind on the bed. Sarah not even calling out at the last moment.

Sarah exalted.

Sarah terribly dead on the top of the damp covers, everything damp and oiled on her, in her.

What had happened to Theo? He was a toehold formed in the sheeting. Sarah, alone, quivered. She could wonder all she liked and it would not matter. The mind chooses for you, what other part is there that could. She was dreadfully thirsty now, after her bath.

32

Dusk and Sarah sat on her quilted bed, braiding her hair. Legs dangling off the end, six pillows propping her, one on her stomach. Bluegrass played hungrily upbeat from her laptop.

She was thinking far away, of how the kindest hour in Manhattan had always been at dusk, when the sun melts the polluted air into a golden-red sprawl and that fierce mechanical quality gives way, appears to give way for a while, to the light of homes, a long quiet breath out, drinks settled and clinked on the tables of outdoor restaurants. And the world is at the right distance.

She had no one at dusk to stop her from taking her shadow for a walk through the East Village, looking in large windows, to steal a little of those other worlds. Wherein pans were being oiled and shaken over flames that lit the face of the chef. And people in black and perfectly rumpled shirts talked with their hands. And private libraries that contained a single elderly gentleman creasing his head over something laid out on his desk, perhaps a life's work, evaluating a complicated perfection. Successful New Yorkers.

Sarah going to the supermarket on C, taking whatever dinners and sometimes a bottle of wine down to the Sixth Street garden where she volunteered on her days off. Sliding the key in the gate. Sometimes there would be others, but usually not. The koi pond black, creased with the streetlights, the fish slurping their reflections as she passed, the water clock keeping its unminuted time.

She would take the oak stairs of the tiny house, the leanness of a watermill in a fairytale. Pass through the upstairs visitors' room – mint-green fleur-de-lis wallpaper, the velvet loveseat, the dollhouse-sized fireplace, the mantle where donated books were kept. Out onto the balcony, to set her meal on the iron-wrought bistro table. Looking down on the trees and the plants that she had helped draw out of the soil. In summer the unbelievable fireflies tracking in their leaves.

But what were those hours of pretence, except failing distilled?

Sarah then, whose moments of happiness had come from fucking a married woman. She was a scrabble of things. But the materials were always there. On solitary watch a rare thing, impenetrable, good.

33

Sarah closed the front door and stepped out, yellow dressed, hair a rope behind. Took a bite out of an apple shining in her hand. Thought a while. The light was clear. Over the way was the cowboy, and it was the idea of him, all the ideas of him she'd had, that finally eased her in to walking that way. High summer was rolling into full splendour, but Sarah had learned that American summer once over is as if it had never been. Like an illness or a holiday, some combination. She walked thinking ominous thoughts about winter. Stopped and threw the core into the grass, walked on.

The cowboy was at the front porch, reading. He looked up. Be wary of that smile.

'Hey.'

'Hello. What are you reading?'

'Nothing world-changing.'

'Well, I suppose not every book needs to be.' Sarah shifted a step to the front door. She tilted her head to read the spine. *Ulysses*. She hadn't read it, but.

'Is your mother in now? I came back.'

'I see you did,' he said. 'I told her about you. Didn't think you'd be two days coming, but that's cool.' Theo rose, taking the book with him.

But I was busy masturbating and panicking, she thought. Forward momentum really wasn't my concern.

They went inside with him in front. The adobe walls were rougher close up, reassuring, cool and dry. Sarah had the sense of intruding upon holy territory. They passed a nook in the wall where a painted metallic form of the virgin stood guard.

'I'm making coffee. You want some?' said the cowboy. He led her into the kitchen. Tossed his book on the table top like it wasn't a mighty brick.

'Yes, please. Coffee.'

There he moved about the room: retrieved coffee from the fridge, opened a cupboard, thumbed a crème-coloured filter from a packet, all with a soft grace. So that Sarah could not help a frisson, which she successfully hid. She had understood the way his body would move.

'So,' Theo began, 'you're here, now.'

'Yes. And so are you.'

His grey tee-shirt, form-fitted, looked well on him. His lips in a bow. His eyes animal, velvet. He filled the glass coffee jug with water. Maybe it would be better if she could look elsewhere. He seemed to acknowledge her looking, but his pace didn't alter.

'I hope you like it, here,' he said. 'You gonna be around a while?'

'Oh yes, it's nice here. Very beautiful.'

'Well,' he said, back turned. He gouged coffee with a metal spoon. 'Well. I mean… so you're going to be here?'

'Um, I think so,' she said. Perhaps he was the controlling type. Or was asking because he and his mother wanted her out, after a while. She was after all just a prickly stranger who had taken over the obnoxious English painter's summer spot, right when the house should be starting down that slow road to decay. The smell of percolating coffee filled the kitchen. He handed her down an earthenware cup and brought out sugar. No one ever translates for you.

'I like the milk warm. It'll take a minute,' he said.

'Sure,' said Sarah, sitting on a chair. How long could she hold a fragment of a smile? She wasn't breathing like herself. She rubbed her right wrist and her fingers. Into the microwave went a squat jug. Earthenware again. Sarah eyed the machine, expecting sparks. Theo stood in the warm kitchen and nothing was said. And if one of them had the advantage it was not clear. The microwave dinged. Sarah drew *Ulysses* towards her, patted it with her hand.

'What a great big monster,' she said. But Theo had nothing

to say to this.

The kitchen around them was cosy: red and yellow, thick-walled and bundles of chillies strung up above an ancient stove. And jams. Lots of them. Clustering by the stovetop newly sealed it looked like, with the labels not yet applied. There was a bundle of labels on the table looking professional. Was the produce made of the strawberries you get in the supermarkets? Or were they genuine. America was obsessed with authenticity, because there is so much that is not quite real. Cartoon impression of fruit and bodies. That attitude rubbing off on her. But even false strawberries are real things, even if they taste of spit. Red enough, livid against the lips.

34

They drank coffee, conversation twitching between them, growing more fluent. The sun arced and began to topple. They talked about books first. Theo loved the stories of Hesse – any aspect of being in the world that could be formed into a clean sort of fable. Sarah wanted to tell him that her favourite short stories were by Gogol. A nobody clerk skitters across an ice-blacked Moscow street hugging his skinny neglected body. He'll never get anywhere other than the absurd territory between his bed and the wall. But Sarah was doubtful Theo would fuck her after that.

And anyway it was summer in the New Mexican high desert, and she was in a sunbeam of a dress and her skin looked good. Theo traced his finger round the lip of his coffee cup. Sarah laid her right hand palm up on the table, and waited for him to trace the broken lines held there. She waited a long time, whispering to herself, you have to touch me, touch me, before we are too much altogether.

35

A lean woman hauled herself in through the kitchen door, carrying a bowl of green-blue eggs which she set in the centre of the table. Sarah withdrew her hand from Theo's.

'Frittata with peppers,' she said, by way of welcome. 'I'm Gam. I'm his mother.'

'Sarah. Good to meet you.'

Gam nodded and picked a skillet off a wall hook.

'You're in Maud's place?'

'I'm her daughter.'

Gam nodded again with her mouth firm.

Frozen bell peppers. Sizzling. Plates appeared, curtly placed on the table. The woman moved about murmuring, instructing herself on what to bring next, the hot touch of handles, ancho peppers, ancho peppers, there. Good.

The frittata appeared, a cream-yellow uneven slab, steaming. A bowl of chili sauce looking like red magma. A salad of leaves – home-grown in the greenhouse on the hill – that had been torn up in the sink, some of the leftover chopped bell peppers, some other things thrown in from just a little too high up. Bacon bits, was Sarah's suspicion.

'So you're in the property cross the road?' Gam asked, getting seated. She scored lines into the frittata. Four portions.

'Yes, that's mine.' As had already been discussed.

'Right, right.'

Sarah watched Gam dole out food. Mother habit, she presumed. A little salad was left over too, a little of the sauce. The older woman looked at the frittata and sighed.

'I'll eat it later,' Theo said, 'let me put it in a tupperware.' He stood and removed the bowls. Cupboards opened. Sounds of plastic being unstacked and clattered. The fridge door clicked. Meanwhile the hot food in front of them steamed and the cold food wilted. And Gam sighed again. It is irritating when a family has practiced its mistakes too long, Sarah thought. You have no map of what to feel for them, but they want you to feel something. She did not have enough of herself to spare for these people. So she picked up her fork and calmly started eating. Gam sighed again and picked through the salad.

'So you're from England?' Said with narrowed eyes.

'Yes, but I've been living in New York for a few years.'

'Yeah, New York, mmhmm,' the woman responded.

Under the cosy overhead light, the yellows and reds on the plate were terrible to behold. But fine, everything tasted fine.

'I'm sorry, we're not used to guests,' Theo said. He smiled that smile you pull out for disasters. The tension in his face threw everything just slightly out of its precision. Theo was at that level of handsome where the surface almost becomes all, almost shuts down the ability of others to pick up on your emotions. Before she had been relying on her excellent conversational skills, but now Sarah let her eyes fall half shut and her shoulders came down a little. Immediately Gam twitched her head.

'What he means to say is you're welcome here any time, any time.' Then, leaning over to briefly pat Sarah's hand, 'Theo's been living here with me the past year, year and a half, and it's not always easy, just the two of us now, but we're doing all right.'

The woman's glass necklace caught the light and sparkled, and the balls of it made a grinding noise. Her black hair was very glossy, cut in a bob, and had been brushed a hundred times every morning, a hundred times at night for years. Sarah smiled back and waited a moment before withdrawing her hand under the table. Her breathing went weird for just a short time.

After dinner, Gam took Sarah out to feed leftovers to her chickens. They went down a dirt, herb-sprung path from the back door to a clump of cottonwoods, where the coop stood, fringed in long fresh grass. Gam got in the chicken yard and shut the mesh door. No entry, it seemed, for Sarah. The woman, ignoring her, tossed a damp scoop of feed and scraps in the direction of the chicken bowls. Sarah flexed her fingers through the wire fence. The hens with lizard eyes peeking, shivering and puffing themselves up from excitement. Though she'd lived in the country, Sarah had never fed a chicken, never been this close. Gam went at throwing scraps steadily so that every bird had its portion. Then, her bowl empty, watched for a while without speaking the dispersal of food, shit, and straw from under their ugly banded feet.

Sarah wondered if Maud and Gam had been friends. The woman sighed, always sighing, and without turning her head, began to speak. Sarah had expected something.

'We're in a bubble right here,' Gam said, 'this property and yours.'

'Oh?'

One bird stepped up the drawbridge into the coop and peered down at them both through the window, gulping and repeating a new kind of anxious movement.

'This land and abouts is protected forest. I don't know how that Browne woman ever got permission to build. Nice lady, your mother, but here's how it is, in my opinion, she ruined that side of the valley. I keep expecting her to put up more houses for summer rents.'

'She won't be doing that,' Sarah said.

'If you're going to stay, if you've taken over, please don't make over there into rentals. It's important to us that the Valle stays calm,' Gam said. As she made to leave the yard, one of the smaller hens shirrup-chirrucked and tried to get out with her.

'No, you,' she told it, pushing it back with her boot and latched the door. 'Sarah, you look like a sensible girl,' she continued, 'you'll think about what I told you, okay?'

Sarah took her cue to say nothing. They walked back up to the house. Gam paused, pointing to a great blue pot full of lavender crawling with bees.

'This here. Could you use some? I know you'll want to get

that garden started back up, soon as you can.'

Sarah pulled off a seedy floret. The scent entered her head raw and steeped in memories so long packed away they'd grown shapeless. If she'd had a grandmother, her grandmother's drawer had smelled like this. In the magazine it had been part of a sacrificial offering, those children with their lavender bundles, their innocent procession through empty, symbol-heavy rooms.

'That would be nice, thank you.'

Gam squatted, stuck her fingers in the potting earth. White roots ripped. And it seemed to Sarah then that Gam was looking at her, without looking at her, as she tore apart the plant. Trailing dirt, and bees flying out and humming, crawling over her ugly chicken-feed slopped sleeves.

'You want this. It'll grow alright. If you know what to do.' Gam got to her feet. Slight pant to her voice. 'If you know the right conditions. Look, I'm going to say it plain. Your mother was a nice woman, real nice. But this place. This place we don't fly off and leave it half the year to be nothing at all.'

Gam seemed to always speak at a quick pace, near thrashing out her words though they were not angry really, and punctuating them with her hands and sighs. Sarah noticed the set dark brown eyes were totally unlike Theo's set dark brown eyes.

Overstaring. Overseeing.

'She's dead, isn't she,' said Gam, glaring back. But again, without any anger. It was unsettling. Sarah nodded without inclining her head.

'Yeah, thought so. Last time... well, it felt like last time,' Gam said.

Saying nothing Sarah held her ground. She let her eyes unfocus. When you are alone in the world you have to do this. For all the years she'd had to. She looked at the withering lavender in Gam's fist. She thought of the spit woman in the bus station toilet. And of Kennedy. All these people and these battening places, and what they make of you, what was she now, and if they realised it didn't take much to make a monster out of a girl.

They reached the door to the kitchen.

'I want to say,' Gam said at last, her hand against the sun-peeled veneer, 'I know what else you're here for. I am not blind and I am well aware. You're looking at Theo. Every girl looks at him. Boys who never looked get second thoughts looking at that face of his. But you just ask him what he does,' the eyebrows up, 'you ask Theo Coronado what he's doing with this life. That's all.'

36

Sarah was back in her cabin listening to the milky way crystallise and explode into brilliant dust above her roof. She flicked the light bulb hanging above her bed: the doorway lurched, and the dimensions of the wardrobe were momentarily terrifying. Sarah vivid as a pin-up girl in a thin, peacock-green newish nightdress, with the straps coming down on her shoulder now and then to remind her of their ease.

She now wanted hot chocolate, sweet hot smoothness, but was too afraid to go downstairs with the lights out. She reached to the bedside table for her phone. It would stop her from falling and splitting open her fragile skull on the stairs. But also help if there was suddenly in the dark another person. No one would be in the dark. No-one; she had read a horror story of a man named No-one. He could come and go as he pleased through stone walls and wood, and liked to watch the unaware through his grey mask. His tongue like the tongue of an anteater, flickering about the mouth-hole.

Sarah clutched at the bannister with one hand, the other tapping buttons on her phone whenever its light threatened to go out. A pallid blue spotlight on the floor that danced her descent.

At the sink in the dimness she poured water over grains of milk. The phone and the licking gas, twin blue light sources. Every motion slowed as if the air was phosphorus-lit water. Her hair floated around her. She popped the lid off the chocolate powder and smelled the contents. It had been in the cabin before her and was of dubious provenance. Still, it was here. She closed her eyes and compared the smell of chocolate to the smell of the lavender plant, which sat, a sodden mess of paper bits and soil, naked on the draining-board.

Sarah, edgeless, sparking, alone.

But of course, she wasn't alone.

Outside she heard tramping. At the back door, she held her cup and looked out towards the forest; nothing moving. Sarah came out onto the porch and peered round the side of her house. There – a lone figure on the grassland, visible beneath a corona moon, was stalking over towards the wood. It stopped. Sarah hurried inside and thumbed some of the switches by the door until the outdoor light went on.

'Hey,' stage-whispered the man, 'sorry, did I wake you?'

It was Theo, it was only Theo, walking towards her. Only, a man she hardly knew, in the middle of the night. Think of the devil. His shade became human under the light that drenched the porch.

37

She wanted to demand what he was doing. Yet could only smile and pour hot milk into his cup. As she drank her own hot chocolate, the liquid found tiny cuts in her lips and burned them. But there is no such thing as an omen or a sign. The universe is not written in a braille we have to learn – both Sarah and Theo could exist as-is, blocks and beads, in the sway of night. Only with the potential for violence lingering on, under the kinder parts of what they told of themselves. Theo against the wall, drinking, smiling. He was being economical, with his words, with the slight angle of his head.

'Have a seat?' asked Sarah, 'us night owls…'

Together on the sofa, the two sipped their drinks and did not speak. The prairie lapped at their back behind glass. The rim road ran hidden where no headlights had broken for a long time and the moon pooled coldly over the whole scene, singling out as far as Sarah could see only the coffee table and the bookcase for a delicate interrogation.

'So, I was told to ask. What is it you do for a living?' Sarah asked.

'I'm an elk counter,' he said.

'You count elk.' Sarah appraised him. 'Really?'

He shifted his eyes to the left. Or she thought he did. Some wetness in them shone and moved left.

'Yup. Part time.' Then he added, 'I look out for the newborns and the dead. Count them and mark it up in a chart. Tag and weigh fawns with the rest of the spring crew. There are herds a thousand head. It's an important job, so they know how many permits to give out to kill them.'

Theo drained his cup, rested his arm against his jeans. Left handed. Sarah looked at the watch on his right. Gold-coloured, oversized; it slid down his wrist, he pushed it back up. Nothing continued to be said.

'Do you treat them, for hoof rot or lameness or—?'

'No. Just births, deaths. I report carcasses and the ranger comes out to inspect.'

Theo turned his watch, let it fall.

'And tonight, where were you going?'

'Going up to check on a cow elk. She's been limping a while, and kinda off on her own. Wanted to see if she's died finally.'

'At this hour?'

'Maybe.' He looked at her. Something rattled at the back of things, and Theo adjusted his posture. Sarah stared at her hands on her lap, remembering she didn't have a bra on, and that Theo was protected in many layers.

'You must know this place like nobody else,' she said, to be hopeful, to permit. Theo was probably not capable of a sudden lunge. Fingers jabbing against her trachea. Of pushing her to the floor against the boards, punching her – cracking cartilage and bone, causing a foam of blood at her lips. Sarah touched her throat lightly.

Too-long pauses as if transmissions from the bottom of the sea. Is everything going to work out okay, do you think. Maybe the pace of New York had ruined her for the country—

'I guess so, I've lived here most my life,' Theo answered.

Without turning her head, Sarah clicked the side lamp on.

'Right. So you'd know what trips I should take around here.'

Theo closed his eyes a moment. 'Yeah, we could talk about that, I guess,' he looked over at her, 'you'll want to see Bandelier.'

'Take off your jacket.'

'Okay.' Theo smiled.

It seemed he did that a lot, but Sarah had noticed how in between the smiling and the poise, he looked as if he was permanently in shadow, and of chilled viscosity like a syrup. There floated into her head the sensation of drawing him in her sketchbook. How she would follow, create, the shape of the shoulders, the profile of the head, the mess of hair. Describe his shape and solidify him. But this was only one way and there were others.

She put her empty mug on the table.

Theo slinked off his jacket. 'Where you want this?'

Sarah said nothing, so he tucked the jacket beside the arm of the sofa. 'Bandelier,' Theo said, 'so it's this ruin southeast of here, in a canyon. Bandelier National Monument. It's kind of famous. Cave dwellings, an abandoned town.'

'Sounds good. Want to go?'

Theo opened his mouth, then shrugged. 'Yeah, I could show you—'

'I have a tent,' she said, rising, 'if we want, we can get out before dawn. Get a head start. You get your stuff together and meet me back here.' She looked at her phone, pleased with the speed of having taken charge. 'Okay, four ten, so shall we say, five?'

Theo got up and allowed himself to be ushered to the door. Had she thrown him at all? Didn't seem so. In a moment he was out and there was no telling if she had averted anything or tried his patience, or if he was confused, or enthusiastic.

Sarah closed the front door gently after him and went to keep watch from the back of the sofa.

Later Theo was coming back, an emblem more or less of various sinister romantic possibilities against the moving sky.

38

Dawn, and the road was cracking through the dry pines, breaking the Rockies down into mesas. Theo sifted through some CDs, though both agreed the day was too tender for music yet.

'Detour? A coffee would go down a treat right now,' Sarah said.

'You're the driver.' Theo gave a friendly stretch. 'There's a gas stop up ahead in like three miles.'

Red mesa flanks, a winding highway. The kind of scene America grants you hardly ever. It was a generous morning. The petrol station appeared around a languorous bend. Sarah turned in and cranked the handbrake. Inside she headed to the ladies. First she checked all the stalls were empty, then she washed her face in icy, strangely silky water from the tap and patted it dry and took out pots and tubes of makeup from her bag and set to work reclaiming what the sleepless night had eroded from her skin.

When she came out, Theo was choosing his coffee. Silence and fine posture. He looked up, caught her eye. He poured himself something called French Colombian. He was handsome, he was young, and he must believe her pretty. Oh and what if he didn't ever tell her? She told herself it all the time in defence against lengthy indifferences and muteness on that point.

'Sugar? Let's go with sugar,' she said. Theo poured a second cup.

By the counter next to the till were clear, flip-lidded containers of various jerkies. Sarah picked out a ragged batwing from one labelled New Mexico Style Green Chili and placed it in one of the small paper bags provided for jerky carriage.

'These, thanks.'

She hardly saw the figure behind the counter, and walking away regretted that blindness. Theo bought a hot tamale, and Sarah wondered where she had heard that phrase before. Hot tamale. A woman who is hot, right. It looked like a big spring roll. Or a well-folded napkin deep fried.

Back in the car, she bit into the jerky – thin, drier than sand, compelling.

'You know, this nasty burnt coffee and vanilla "crème" and these salty, spicy bits of… pterodactyl skin,' she flapped the jerky bag, 'this is the most delicious breakfast imaginable.'

Theo laughed. Short, light. Not much given. 'Wanna bite of mine?'

He was sitting in his seat, both feet curled beneath him, binding the knees together with his arms. He took off his shoes, his jumper; he took off his several layers of irony and care. He came to look like an overgrown boy, that gold watch bigger than ever on his wrist.

'No, no. It looks like… like a deep fried napkin,' she had to say.

The car drove off down the whitened asphalt, and everything was easy. Just for breakfast, and maybe afterwards, for the length of a few songs.

The most beautiful place she had seen was a land crossed while under the influence of a blank disgust where love and her crimes were seared away from her. That most beautiful place, it was in Devon, passed through solo on foot pushing her bike, an open field with hard furrows and a pale sky and her breath ghosting in front. She took sterile to be best. When she forgot her body that was best. When she had amnesia about her insides and membranes separating them from the outside, and was walking somewhere unimportant, let's say, just right after she had very deliberately slit her mother's hand and had to be restrained from slitting worse, and had left home and known exactly who she was and what she had grown to be. Her hand had ached. She kept forgetfully licking her teeth and pressing her hand which meant re-wrapping it every few miles or so. This was the beautiful place. All around. A halo of it, separating her from her from herself.

When you wield a shard of glass it cuts you too, and the nerve endings tingle under the bandage and you have a cool duffle coat on and green tights. A tender age, you walk up into the afternoon light over the hills, a shortcut, maybe there's a barn to sleep in. You are prepared to do away with yourself, but will avoid that for the time being while the kind English hills absolve you. Until they don't and you need a changed landscape. A fresh continent, if the old is that seeped through and encrusted. That's the point. To walk forever being forgiven by whatever's outside because your insides keep leaking your disgust and that holds you together, keeps you from sin and from washing away and you cannot ever go home. Onward without ceasing, sullen steady-footed. Don't touch it, it still won't have healed. Blood wooze. Wouldn't it be nice to have a tea a short sit down.

The air lay sweet and still in the flat mouth of the canyon. A chik-chik from above, where the sun was glinting through high desert pine. Theo and Sarah got out of the car and walked through the empty visitors' centre, where a covered passage separated the part of the canyon given over to the road and the forested car park from the sanctuary beyond.

'We got here early,' Theo said. 'We'll be the only ones awhile. Until it opens for real.'

Sarah pushed a set of double doors and they were out into the light-drenched, sheltered world. A black path wound ahead towards one pink sand-toned cliff wall. Metal plaques along the way depicted the silhouettes of trees and prominent lizards and birds. Little white squares were numbered to correspond to notes in a booklet Theo had taken from a stand: here was a cooking stove, there a cornfield, elsewhere a place where traded quarry stone had been found. Sarah glanced about, but there was nothing to be seen but fallow and cottonwood trees. Eventually they came to a circle that had been a walled village and a sunken kiva with the roof long dismantled. Sarah looking curiously at things but mostly letting herself be dumb. Moving along the day's broad beam, at the side of this man, through this sweet morning air.

The path took them upwards, below the high shadowed mouths of ancient dwellings hand-carved into the canyon's tuff walls. Sarah clambered up the display ladder to peer into a fired chamber.

The black round room was a pod, a cell. Had they all lived in communal solitude, a domed cave each?

'You should come up,' she called down.

Theo hesitated. Sarah sat alone in the cell. Looked beyond across the dry valley to the silenced village ruin occupying the centre. Over against the further side of the canyon were green thickets, swaying mildly. A stream threaded them together.

European invaders once came shrugging in on horseback down the steep pathless routes, squinting, patting their guns, their ornate sabres. Imagine the bastards' surprise. Ghost town already. A raven slashed out a little territory overhead.

'Are you coming up?' Sarah thought perhaps she didn't want him now.

'Yeah, one sec.'

A hand appeared, and another. Theo swung himself in, he could just move like that, graceful and unstoppable. Two people filled the cavern with their knees and elbows. Sarah shifted herself into one corner, imagining a way of inhabiting the room that would not involve constraints.

'I guess it's single occupancy only,' said Theo.

They briefly watched the view as if they ought to.

'What do you think these people did, when they wanted company?'

'I think,' said Theo, looking at her, looking very much at her, 'I think they would call down, and the other would come up, push the curtain back and come into the room. Without space to move, they'd have to really know what it was they wanted.'

True, she thought. Space creates distance and necessitates performance. Because of subtleties, misreadings proliferate.

'I don't think they would have had a plan,' Sarah said, 'perhaps it just happened they were here together, or they had something to discuss,' she leaned in and whispered, 'conspirators.'

'Yeah, and do you think we are conspiring?' asked Theo.

Sarah pushed close and kissed him. That's how it works, you crank the handle and the thing plays out. Stubble, hot meat-spiced breath. She closed her eyes. She felt cave crumbling under her fingernails. It was soft shell, it was old foundation. Theo's hands were between the thighs of her jeans. Rubbing as her tongue pressed into his mouth. She moaned, and his skin smelled of salt and sleeplessness.

This carried them, a while. All this was delightful, but. The muzzle of conflicted feeling at her throat. She pushed Theo back. Lips broke and left open.

'I'm sorry—' Sarah said.

'No—' said Theo.

Breathing heavy, the two tidied their hair, dusted themselves off. And tried not to feel the sun that was a splash of hot now, on bodies also hot, descended the ladder into the luxury and pressure of the open canyon.

41

Sarah thought outdoor thoughts. Drifting down the path, lungfuls of air and of being in the sun, the body of the boy ahead, the silence of dry trees and small darting animals. Gradually her thoughts coalesced into thinking of how she had kept love for Kennedy in her heart. Like water. That was the clearest metaphor.

Water in the chambers of her heart – a heart, which she reminded herself, was like a slimy fist in her chest clutching only at itself – where it had boiled and thundered and fed nothing. Leached at her too. There were channels and caverns inside her. Blind salamander lived there, evolved to dwell without light. The hollows were what had held her back. They had given her a unique reverb. She really did enjoy the image, turned it over and over. The morning anyway was very beautiful. She began to think again in the outdoor way.

'It's peaceful,' Theo said, still walking ahead. Warming asphalt underfoot, the going easy. Then they were silent all the more.

On the way out they read a sign on the path which explained that in the early twentieth century a small family hotel had been set up in this canyon, at a time when the only access was from the mesa top above by rope ladder. And all around was only soaring black birds and ruined cornfields. What a charmingly insouciant and invasive thing to do. When national monument status was granted the hotel was torn down and the family left, grateful the valley and its heritage would be preserved in perpetuity, is what the sign said.

The woman who'd run the hotel had kept a herb garden, coaxed vegetables and fruit trees in order to feed her patrons, to claim herself here. But the trees had been cut down and burned and their ashes salted, because now only native species were allowed in the park. Did Sarah have any way of reasoning with this narrative? She hung back, looking at the stones in the ground, imagining a Hotel Browne. Sarah in a woman's work dress from the thirties. Her dark hair bound back with cotton cloth. Hoe in hand, posing for a photograph. Serious, or smiling? Broad smile. Assured of her place, with no one else to counter. The weight of a homegrown peach in a calloused hand. No one else, nothing but that specific, gentle kind of contact, that imagined, tender flesh.

Into the car park. A roil of hot dogs and stew – posole, Theo said – came off the visitor centre café. Insects were now awake and playing between the pine branches and the leaf drift. Sarah wished she could live like them, stick herself to a mate, to dance, an ooze of pollen and insectual fluids, then to split apart, deseaming, done. But mostly she could do that. It was more to have their fabulous eyes and mechanical methods of approach.

In the car the hot plastic interior smelled of breakfast. The metal parts of the seatbelts blazed silver and liquid. Sarah with her tongue like a drumlin in her mouth lowered the windows, rolled the car onto the road up and out; from the corner of her eye watching dark-eyed Theo's hair thrash, getting further dishevelled. Out they flew, out of the mouth of the valley and up onto the topside mesa road.

Emerging from the long grass into the floodlight was a dust-grey dog with a lithe step. It was Sarah's first coyote. Sarah, toothbrush in hand, towel bundled underarm. The coyote in its fur, staring. A long time holding her there, wiser and colder than the stray in Oklahoma. Why was it the animals? But she didn't bother completing the thought.

'Sorry, I've eaten all my dinner,' Sarah said. They'd had smoky charred steaks, toothsome and unctuous, sweet potatoes wrapped and set amongst the coals then mashed in their skins with butter and salt. Plastic plates greasy, streaked with ashy finger prints. Theo had sat across from her, absorbed in his firelit book. Turning the pages delicately, knowing she looked on. The two of them not tense. Perhaps tense. Pre-emptivity weighs on us all these days.

She looked up at the stars. Are there even stars in the twenty-first century? She remembered reading a witty comment: your eyes are like stars, they are already dead. What a turgid lyric to think of. At no time should you emulate anything that might be sung by a scrawny white boy in a beanie with an ear gauge. She took a step back on her heel. The coyote made a smooth dart back into the grass. Sarah walked on towards the shower block. She passed a stink beetle resting its head against concrete. Shiny black like a gun, like a purse swollen with imminent disgust.

44

There's something about men and how they expect you after a time to curdle or else they await your hatred with a horse's gross wet eyes, or they don't even know what's hit them when it does. And women were not at all any different. Only that they recognised things quicker. Of course being Sarah she could see that everything she thought regarding men versus women were just her grabby assumptions crumpled together like old dollars. Or I-owe-yous to herself. That was her superpower. To be aware of instances of cliché and to embrace them, the fragility of them, for want of anything more convincing. No irony for you. Irony is a luxury for those who think the truth is their right, they just don't got it yet. As for Sarah. A little flick of the sunglasses and you live. That is glamour. How is it, by the way, her life failed the Bechdel test? Well. Fuck. That would be because she didn't have any friends, or at least could not remember if she did. A collection of email addresses preserved on account. Friendless, motherless, sharply beautiful, embrace that.

There's something about being placeless that precludes thinking of ghost villages and abandonment without a strange sense of achievement.

In the washroom, a prefab box of light, Sarah stood naked and shuddery. The cold water prickled then burned hot against her spine. It was quiet, just the sounds of her splashing. The water puddled in the blue shower tray, slopping as Sarah turned her feet. Bothersome moths whisked overhead, flirting stupidly with the light bulb. Someone came in, made the floor panels creak, clattering a stall lock. Then the flush and taps squeaking, and the grunt of the outside door shutting shook the walls. And then the space was hers again.

She imagined Theo waiting for her like a stranger sitting in a shelter on a lonely railway platform. Snow falling for months and miles. There was a sense of rabbit fur cloaks and mustard-coloured valises. There was a sense of a train coming in on schedule, for all the reluctance of the weather. She flicked an eyelash from her belly, she tilted her head right back to give her throat to the water.

On the walk back by silent plots, her shorts rode up on her. The warmth had gone and she would have to put on ugly socks. A little distant from their campsite she stopped to let the night and the wilderness swarm her under the stars. Ahead the flank of a silver Airstream caravan. Gingham curtain. And the scent of everything and the dark of everything, how all-encompassing and to be fought.

Sarah slipped off her shoes and lined them up at the entrance, unzipped the door and folded herself inside.

'Hey. You get lost?' asked Theo. He had made a nest in his sleeping bag, the corner of a thin book poking out. Glossy shadows like treacle banding his lap, his sides. And his molten eyes were watching her. His mouth full and feminine in the soft light.

Sarah snaked into her bag, flipping the hood up, tugging the drawstrings all the way.

'I got into a stand-off with a coyote,' she said.

'How did it go?'

'It was kind of prickly with me. I must have let it down somehow.'

Theo dropped his book. Sarah wondered briefly if he had finished or abandoned *Ulysses*, and hoped for the latter. Copying her, he raised his own hood and pulled the toggle to his throat. A young monk.

'Well, I wouldn't worry too much. Can't believe animals take an interest in us, no matter how much we impact their lives.'

'Well, I wouldn't. I mean, take an interest in me.'

'Didn't you just move out here, on your own, from New York City? You grew up in England, right?'

'Yes...'

'Maud said she...' A pause. 'I guess you got nothing of interest to tell me.'

Sarah shifted. She'd heard that before. A dark blue something hulked by outside the tent cracking twigs. Someone looking for a spot to pee in. Some monster hungry for kinship. Theo's blank curiosity. She had the urge to flee but damped that down. She didn't have to be anything but to herself an armoured girl biting down on her shield.

'Nothing of interest to you or coyotes.' And zipped her arms out of the sleeping bag, reached for his book. Grey cover, no title. She flicked through it, but it was in Spanish. Some time passed before she looked at him again; under the padded hood, his thin brows sat low. He stared at nothing a while but never looked frightened. It was exhaustion, maybe.

I've made myself, Sarah wanted to tell him. I clawed out of a picture and made my own body and my shitty life and obsessions. She reached over and pulled down the zip on his sleeping bag, to just below his solar plexus. He had taken off his shirt when she had been out. Shadows sweeping downwards in gradations. She pressed her thumb against his collar bone, where the first few hairs began.

I could hurt you more than you could hurt me.

Theo was holding his breath.

'Here,' Sarah heard herself saying, 'come here.'

They pushed their tired lips together.

The black grandeur of the park. The salt-grey embers of the fire outside. Their tent, a half-globe of blueish light. Nearly nothing, in the scale of things. Inside Sarah held her eyes closed. Thought nothing until she was. The two lovers moved together and were.

A tremulous cold invaded just after dawn. Sarah shifted to touch the sleeping body in its separate sack. It gave a small moan and the legs drew up, protecting. All character concealed by sleep. If she had a thermometer she'd be able to tell the temperature, but it felt below zero. Minus two or three. There was the finest condensation suspended on the walls. The water bottle was full of slush.

Outside morning voices. Crackling, clanking noises. The smell of wood fire, coffee. Sarah opened the larger door to air the tent and peeked out. A black squirrel was shimmying up the trunk of a juniper tree. Pausing intermittently, flicking its head like a small lizard, until it circled too high to view.

Sarah clambered out to find a flat dry stone on which to sit in the coming sun.

Kennedy never referred to herself by her first name, listed it even on the volunteer register and on credit cards as 'E'.

Elizabeth (for such a preppy sort) or
Emily
Evelyn
Eleanor
Euphemia or
Eukulele

Sarah guessed, never correct. But never googled either.

'Fuck, how rude of me,' Kennedy had said, chopping at some earth, at stone, mighty that way. 'You know I'm not well-bred.'

'You went to a private school, Kennedy. That's the definition. So people say.'

'Yeah, well. I believe in well-bred, and I'm not it. Fuck that. Wanna know what I learned at my prep school before they threw my ass out of there? How to make full use of the privileges of my class while not acknowledging them as such.'

Kennedy had been to college, Sarah thought, and dropped out after meeting her husband – probably ten years older and who chucked her under the chin when she was like this. Aren't we better people when we don't theorise ourselves, he'd probably say.

'And they kicked you out. That you say is your refutation,' Sarah had said, 'your life is a refutation of upper class values.'

'That's right, that's right,' Kennedy slapped the earth with satisfaction, 'we both got out, and here we are.' She had laughed.

Sarah had merely smiled and snipped back at weeds. If she spoke, she was sure to say something too revealing.

Kennedy's tweed trousers, as she crouched and fanned and

wiped her hands. That red silk blouse gaping to show off her breasts. The tiny sweat stains under the arms, though she hardly seemed to notice the heat. Did people like this really exist? Sarah believed it to be that kind of glamour, that honest overconfidence grown only in America. Something you could almost take for truth and essential. Replicable with the right earrings, the right delicate intertwining floral tattoos.

Theo was dressed and busy packing the tent into its cover when Sarah returned. She helped load the gear into the boot and took one last survey of the site. Which meant kicking gravel and staring off into space.

'Last night,' began Theo, leaning his back against the car. He seemed steady. The skin under his eyes would feel like a peach on the turn. Pulpy, unless you took care.

'Hmm,' Sarah said, and dusted the lower legs of her jeans. It occurred to her they hadn't left enough firewood for the next campers. She wandered off the pitch into the bush. Theo followed after.

'You don't want to talk?'

'No. I wouldn't. I'm not – full of words. Not that it wasn't, you know, quite lovely.' She threw a few sticks on the pile and stamped down on the dead wood. She remembered to glance up at him and give a half smile.

'Fine,' Theo said. 'Guess if that's all it was, then I'm still glad.' And he smiled back slightly too. More generously than she had.

Of course that wasn't all there was to it. Driving off the mesa top, breezes came in the open windows louder than anything, and the sun hid beneath the pine, and was far more tender and reproachful than either of them deserved.

Weeks had been filled and filed off somewhere.

Calls to her bank the lawyers in the UK tedious swift guilty provisions trips to Esta

walks along the valley sides

emails to Kennedy almost sent, deleted

lustrous afternoon sulks

creature watching. Prairie dog burrows and spry bluebirds from Colorado on the other side of the mountains

long showers

preparing and eating dinner silently or with emphatic theme music

firelit stays reading and sketching

having the immense empty day tell its various stories of her murder and death, of her murdering and killing, being triumphant over these fantasies

meeting with Theo, still desired and still unsatiating, usually after dark when the moon drew the clouds to itself by magnetic power, and the land heaved

Charging afterwards into the cooling white mornings.

One evening Theo invited Sarah out onto the Coronados' roof. They sat together waiting on the cooling of the adobe flat top. Until there were enough stars to prompt awe and kindness. Theo leaned with his back to the low guard-wall. Habitually at ease, legs stretched out, boots crossed. It irritated her.

She thought of all the things love was supposed to be. In poems and in art, it flows. That's the singular thing she could get in the whole universality of love – fucking slipperiness. If only she and Kennedy had both wanted love. Or if their fucking had been hard enough, if they could have been that good. Her and Kennedy, her and Theo. Sarah needed and needed and rasped away. Love was a shiny surface she could never grasp. She peeled open constantly like a boiling star. She was dead like a star and she could not give up.

A smell hung in the night air of plaster-of-paris and something bright like mint oil. Down in her bedroom Gam was listening to a talent contest on the TV. The applause and hoots coming out staccato between bursts of earnestness. It formed a strange punctuation to their quiet talk.

'And now?' Theo said.

'Not anything different from the last time you asked.'

Theo gave a slight, wounded sigh. Pulled her close by her elbow. Awkward, but it was the only part he could reach.

'Well, I guess I can't stop wanting there to be. I really can't,' he said. 'I guess there is nothing I can do. There was some asshole guy, right, in New York? I'll listen. If you want. I'll drive with you down to the border and cross it at dawn and buy you tequila at 10am. Whatever you want.'

Theo pushed his head against hers, against her neck. Lover, love, I love you, fuck. His hair tickled her cheek and it was the down of a goose, it was enough to throw a person from themselves if done right.

There was a cold coin in her brain that would not dissolve. I am not this, it said. Engraved on copper as Theo pulled his head up and kissed her. Copper in her skull tanged against the cells. Sending a pulse outwards of electrical dismay.

And Theo nipping at her neck.

And Sarah plunging her hands up under his tee-shirt.

And Sarah cursing softly.

Do other people sense the withholding of another? Why could Theo not feel it? Theo was a room lit in a far-off house. Theo was a wisp going over a marsh, chattering to itself. He was kneading her breasts and breathing in her mouth.

'I want to—' Sarah began, but there was no finish. She wanted, she wanted.

She dragged down the zipper of his jeans.

52

Theo washed his hands and wrists like a surgeon. He had been at the cabin for an hour and had methodically built Sarah a fire in the stove. But now the blaze was going and the man was peaceful. The day had been full of storms and howls outside. Sarah was working in grey charcoal and yellow ink, scratching out a landscape. Theo shrugged up against a cabinet. She sly-eyed his handsomeness as he flicked through a stack of info pamphlets. He did like to prop himself on things. If Sarah had to guess the harshest reason why, it was that he did not like to let things have chance to attack him from behind. But that was a bit much to suppose.

Above him hung a photograph of a field at dawn in some winter, the only picture she'd left up of Maud's. A Cornish field it would be. She thought of winter in New York and an image came to her, of a stretch of East Houston Street frozen solid and, stuck together in the ice, a dog turd and receipt for a fancy supermarket listing kombucha, blue cornmeal chips, a fifty-dollar bouquet of flowers.

She wondered if it would be all right to ask Theo if he had these ugly moments of interconnectivity. Or, instead to say, you know how the light from the sun takes eight minutes to reach us? Well if our star suddenly died we wouldn't know immediately. That delay is where we live out our time. Imagine the world service newscaster, addressing everyone who still listen to the world service:

I am sorry to inform you that our sun has gone out. We have six minutes left of this light.

I love you, world.

I am a sentimental chap but there you are. We are permitted to be sentimental now and tears are the best ritual. We should seek to be soothed, not forgiven. Into the dark we must go.

Sarah shook herself out of this.

'So, Theo,' she asked, 'is there any other place you think I should see around here?' Her voice had a creak in it, like an affectation.

'Why, you bored?'

'No?'

'Everything is a question when you say it,' his heavy head of curls and his eyes low, 'can't get a grip on your thinking sometimes.'

Sarah put the lid on her ink bottle and screwed her brushes in an oiled rag and put them away in their case. And did not sigh.

'I'm not doubtful,' she said at last, 'I am full of questions. Like about this place. You.'

She went to the sofa. Conciliatory moves begin with pretending you are physically comfortable yourself. After a while Theo came over and sat beside her, slid his head into her lap.

'Tell me,' she said, 'why you're living here.'

'That'll take some time,' he began. 'Why live here? The short of it is I had a job, in Albuquerque. Was happy with all of it. I worked as a technician at a college library. At night, I was taking veterinary courses, they gave me staff rates. I had my own place. I had friends.'

Sarah was stroking his hair though it took her a moment to realise she was doing so. And that they were breathing together. She moved her hand to her side and pursed her mouth.

'It always starts out so hopeful…'

'Mmm. They cut my job out, merged it with another, something like that. I had to come back here after six months looking for work elsewhere. I helped Gam out with the business. She was fine with having me home, so I guess I was lucky. If we didn't get on well, I might've had nowhere to go. Maybe—'

'What about your friends?'

'Well, it's hard to keep things going when you only have

hardship in common. I found that out.'

'Yes,' said Sarah, 'I'd like to think that wouldn't be true of every friendship, but same here. Only it was my own fault. I just stopped talking to people, or returning their emails. After leaving, they didn't exist.'

A lie.

'Yeah, maybe that was me too. Or just. Whatever. Messy time.'

Theo yawned. A snap from the fire. It was late, and how comfortable they were, Sarah thought. They talked on about past derailment and never about what might come next.

'My brother—' Theo began, but stopped himself. Or something caught. Clearly this was for another day. And anyway tragedies are boring and ruin the mood. Theo twisted his watch. He took a few gulps and neither of them spoke. Sarah began stroking his hair again, though thinking she really shouldn't.

The house clicked to remind them it was there, decaying. After a while Sarah sat forward, and Theo moved to sink behind her, curling up his legs. Soon his breath was low and even. She pulled the blanket down on him. Stayed beside him for an unmeasured period of time, basking in the glamour of being the only conscious creature in the house, in the nestle of the mountains, on this brief side of wakefulness.

What she would spend her money on

She would buy him a small upright house in Albuquerque. With a garden that was dry and filled with zen swirls and river pebbles. She would pay for his vet course. Better to be kept by a fallible human than by a loan company that suckles like a tick until it bloats. She would say, your debt is to love for a limited time until we part. Whatever, we can call it love or something else. Had philosophers given it an old Greek name?

And after she was done, she would buy herself a ticket for home. For her own homeland and the solitude that came parcelled in ways she had down: sea air and dewy grass that never dried out and the St Mawes men in The Arms gnarling happily into their pints. Well of course she had an émigré's view of home. But that would easily be undone. Like a shoelace, like a debt unfleshed.

Her money would pick them both free. Their bodies shining, immaculate of backstory. And then after that. She would make sure that her life would no longer be a sentence fragment or shackled to metaphors, but a steady drawing forward and one day back, back home.

53

Sarah tiptoed to the bathroom, arms outstretched, grazing the tips of her fingers against surfaces porcelain-cold and wood-warm. And wondered what had drugged her. Blood was up like sap, or like oxygen churning white in a waterfall. She had slept for only three hours. What sweet water flows in sleep. She was going to start giggling soon, this must stop.

She changed into a tee-shirt and a pair of lightweight athletics trousers, calming, rusted shades good for the Autumn weather. She put on a musky amber perfume. Back downstairs Theodore Coronado was asleep on the sofa under the tweed blanket. A head of curls and soft corners. She could say, come, wake up, fuck me now. She had a friend. She had a confidant. Only, she wasn't going to tell him about the millions. Just pick out an Albuquerque home, very nice very darling, and put his name on the front door for him.

Theo must have heard her garbled thoughts: he stirred and jolted upright, crumpling the blanket and pushing himself off the sofa.

'Shit, what time is it?'

'Early. Would you like some breakfast?'

'No, I asked what time is it? I got to be someplace.'

'Well, I think it's about seven thirty.'

'You think?' Theo said, twisting into his clothes.

'Okay, seven forty-three precisely. The clock's right there.'

'Shit. I'm so sorry, Sarah, I have to go. I'm supposed to see someone today.'

Sarah moved aside as he ran about gathering his things. She sat at the counter as he put on his socks and shoes scowling and mumbling to himself.

'You look like a politician about to be caught in a scandal,' she said.

'What?' he said.

'I said—'

'Yeah, I heard. It's "what" because that was a really weird thing to say.'

'A joke. Actually, my father was a Japanese-American politician. Not, like, a senator or anything—'

'Right. Anyway. I got to go.'

When Sarah made motions to continue, he pressed his finger to her lips, 'Later, okay?'

The door clattered behind him.

Sarah had been stupid. Dreaming of a companionable morning eating toast and sipping on rank cabin coffee. Theo helping her after to dry the dishes, maybe even his arms loosely around her waist.

'Fuck. All right,' she said aloud, 'well anyway.' She brought her hands together in a sharp clap, as if to smash an insect. She noted the room echoing at the sound of the clap, and that sound dying away. She would go into town. Collect a few things. Find the Esta library, pick up a copy of *Ulysses*.

Set with a plan, Sarah made some toast, and to go with it a jam labelled strawberry which she found in the cupboard above the sink. It had, like all these other secret foods, come with the cabin and was maybe a hundred and fifty years old. No, max, two years, which was likely the last time Maud had been well enough to come over, according to Cousin Lucy. The contents of the jar had a glistening pinkish surface a little cracked, with denser blobs within it like lumps of boiled fleshy tissue. Anyway. She scraped a little over the toast, making a strange, loud noise in the emptiness. The lumps would not be broken down flat. Sarah bit into her breakfast. There was an unfamiliar sickly note to the taste, not sugar, not strawberry. It could be corn syrup, which was in everything here.

She poured herself a glass of water and watched half the coated toast grow cold and uneaten on the brown plate. She rubbed her sticky hands on the wooden counter and left.

You must buy food to eat and feel strong, she told herself holding a can of tuna. Even if she had a limited budget until the money was processed and came in, she still had to put food in her body. Chicken of the Sea though, what a horrifying name. She put it in her basket. One day all the tuna would be gone. Better have some while it was still there to be had. She picked out a banana that miraculously was ripe. Telling herself she needed the potassium, whatever potassium was for.

Sarah stowed the shopping in the car and went off to find the public library, planning to eat her banana on the way. But she had an oily, sour taste in her mouth and could not. She felt knackered too, the missed sleep finally hitting her. When she came to it the library was shut up like a mortuary. Beside it was a German 'Ubermart', outside of which a man in butcher's whites and striped apron was handing out samples in small paper cups. She gave him a disgusted look and went into a nondescript building next door, which turned out to be both a pharmacy and a place to renew car licences. The woman at the counter was clenched up and dreary. There was a grey carpet, smudgy windows too dirty to see out of.

Sarah sat down in a cherry-red bucket chair and had a staring contest with a poster showing a young man filling in a form of some kind. His pencil balanced forever over a piece of paper with nothing on it. There was a Wi-Fi signal on her phone. Sarah's own pose so desolate that no one bothered her as she looked up her emails.

There was one dated a few weeks back, from Kennedy.

RE:
No more, right hun? U r embarrassing me.
We are done. Your a smart girl, u no that.

That was it in full. Somehow the emails she'd composed in her head had got through without her having to type and send, wasn't that just the way. To be the inverse of psychic. Spreading your thoughts at people like grotty spores. Sarah sighed. Her hands fell. All this weirdness was just like Kennedy. After a moment she rolled the cursor over the delete option. If she clicked, it would go away. As if it had never been written.

Keep it then for a time. For all time, forever, as long as her account existed, the email server retained its cache. She could think of it as a missive from God, telling her, after all those unformed, scrunched up prayers, see child – she really did get kicked out of high school.

What she would spend her money on

She would buy the most English building she could think of and have it installed in the Valle Grande. To transport a castle stone by stone wouldn't do because to import a castle and pretend to be a noble was a particularly American activity: she would out of all possible choices build an electricity substation and disguise it as a townhouse, but with sinister false windows so that people would pass in wonder at this piece of London architecture sitting in the midst of a mountain valley and shiver.

'Nobody ever goes in, nobody ever comes out,' it would utter cleverly to itself. But that would be a recording, played on infinite loop. There would be ducts and wires but nothing would hook up to anything else. And in the centre of the house would be a bottle of gin filled with gummy sweets with a label that would say keep out, fuck off. But also there would hang a small hammer in glass nearby which said only joking, help yourself. And when you broke the gin bottle it would smell briefly of walking home from a club on a Sunday morning in a small blinking rain.

56

Sarah vomited into an abandoned tire and then wiped her mouth with her sleeve. On the drive home that creeping unwell feeling had bloomed into nausea, intensifying on each turn. Now she stood looking in a pink-tinged ditch by the side of the road. She stepped a little way into the pines, stomach still cramping. The jam, she thought. What were the symptoms of botulism again? And what should she do? Go back to the pharmacy? She spat into the grass. Go home and double up over the toilet. Wasn't the air good out here though.

Pain, and hot sour mouth. Please let it not be botulism. She didn't have the money to spare, not yet. The Coronado family, they might have some pharmaceuticals. Sarah lowered herself into the driver's seat. Not too far to go, just a handful of turns.

Sweating and heavy eyed. There, finally there was the house. She parked across their drive, opened the door, staggered a short way, and threw up violently at the foot of a withered tree. There was a rope twisting above her. Remnant of an old swing.

Sarah knocked at the door and held her head against a porch beam, waiting for some minutes until no one came.

She dragged herself away from the post and walked around the side of the house. The path to the left went to the chickens – though the coop was hidden, Sarah was sure she could smell them. All those chicken-bodies, scraped chicken shit. She called out for Theo, for Gam. No one answered.

The path ahead inclined into the hills. Gam had mentioned a greenhouse up there. Sarah wiped her clammy face and walked on. A commune of trees stood with their arms reaching, the grass between them cut and cleared, and beyond them an elegant glass building with green-tinted panes. Although it was not close to dusk a bright light shone from the greenhouse, and there was music. Operatic and loud as she pushed in. The air pushed back steamy, green, illicit. She staggered by a row of tall, jaunty plants. Glossy and jagged, with seven-fingered leaves. She pulled off a tester leaf for her pocket, squashing it a little between her heavy fingers. Facing away from the door sat Gam, bent over a little lamp-lit desk. And immediately noticeable an electronic silver plate scale.

A free standing fan rotated in the corner chopping the air. Sarah listened, hypnotised a while.

'Mmm...' she said, finally.

Gam turned herself around on her chair slowly.

'Oh girl, huh, you don't look well. You looking for me?'

Sarah nodded, and vomited for a third time into the leaves of the nearest cannabis bush.

57

The wonders of consumer-led medicine. They had liquids that made you throw up. You just buy a big bottle of the vomit inducer and take it home and have a good time. Then you chase that with milk of magnesium or whatever brand name it had, the pink stuff, to soothe you afterwards. And electrolyte replacement sachets and plenty of fluids and stern admonishments and rolled eyes and a chunk of money, which Gam, of all people, had paid. That was the worst of it over, Sarah had thought. But it wasn't.

'Now, getting to the real issue,' Gam said as she drove Sarah home.

'What's that? Ah shit,' Sarah lolled in the passenger side trying hard not to drop her bag of medicines. Then scrabbling for them when she did. The electrolyte stuff looked like a packet of instant gelatine.

'Sarah, are you listening? Tell me how you got sick.'

'Food poisoning. That's what the doctor thought anyway,' Sarah said. She wondered if some of her teeth had crumbled from the bile wash. Molars like sandcastles. And then Gam peered over at her.

'That's what he said. What he thought. On what? No evidence. It could be something else you know.'

Worms.

Tropical virus.

But it was pregnancy, that's what Gam thought. Sarah was too tired to care. Let her think whatever. Let her.

Gam parked on the verge by her driveway. Sarah's car had to be moved to let her get in, but first this important conversation was going to happen.

Sarah let her face go slack. If only she had her sunglasses on. That would be the right level of disdain.

'I just think you need to get a test,' Gam said. She got out of her car to open the passenger door for Sarah. Pause for thought. Pause for the flourish. 'I know, I can get you groceries later and bring over a test then. It's good to check, right? For all of us. Plus you get groceries.'

Gam's gaze like a lizard. A lizard's infrequent, wet blinks.

'No, no,' Sarah said, getting out, 'thank you for helping me, I greatly appreciate it. I just have to go home now. If I need help, Theo's a phone call away.' She got into her own safe powder blue rental car. 'He can always bring me a little bag of your weed to get me eating again.'

Gam's face moved about in an interesting way. When people have something harsh they can't say outright it's always interesting to watch. Sarah drove off, seeing lizard Gam get smaller and more desiccated in the rear-view mirror, till she turned into a stump of blasted pine, an inch of tarmac, a big pacific field of valley grass.

58

Sarah turned the engine off. Listened to the mild ticking noise of cooling and the sound of insects blipping against the windshield. She thought of the security guard at the motel in Santa Fe. She wondered if she would ever return her rented car. Deposit: $400, Santa Fe auto hire. She was keeping it till they sent someone out to drag it back.

She tilted back the seat and closed her eyes. She dreamed of her mother's skin smelling of oats and viola odorata, of being very young and held close. Parma violets. Beeswax and linseed oil, textures more than smells. She woke mushy headed with her tongue stuck to the floor of her mouth. She shifted and gazed out blankly and wished she was home.

What on earth could she have meant by that?

How lonely it had made her as a child, when her mother had left her, away to this cabin probably. And how much worse it was when on her mother's return there was that single hug and one smile doled out. At the back door of the Warne, at the airport gates. Sardonic, if Sarah lingered, even a little bit.

It occurred to her that she spent too much time reducing the imposing, discordant energy of her mother to a pocket-sized river pebble. She was trying to make her childhood easier to hold. But it did not matter at all what she thought. Fuck everything tender. Throw all mothers in a hole in the ground and piss in it. And in after them go the boyfriends who pine and shrug and leave. And the girlfriends who laugh at their own daring or are never there or were never really your girlfriend, just a slip-stepped demon you hugged too tight. After that drown the lot in kerosene and chuck in a handful of matches lit all at once. Smouldering graves, burnt land, burnt bridges. Put up a barrow that says nothing on it to date or clarify.

Sarah bleared out the window. Oh bravado. She sighed and

got out of the car. Walked upstairs to the bathroom and looked at her puffy face all scored over with pressure lines. It was a pleasing face, otherwise. She drank water from her cupped hands and brushed her teeth. She had come out here to get her life in order and that is what she would do. Her reflection, the light hitting the bathroom wall, made her face into an icon and showed the limits of failure had nothing at all on her resplendence.

59

It was time to embark on a project. Sarah pulled out her sketchbook and flitted through the disjointed images of horror crows and looming elk and branches. She needed to construct something metaphysical. Or aerial, tactile. It would come clear in the doing. Though she would have preferred a big milky tea, she downed a cup of black coffee like a pro. She slipped a Swiss Army knife from the cutlery drawer. Then she went upstairs to the bedroom and picked out an outfit from the wardrobe: a sky blue shirt bought in a Salvation Army store, a pair of dark jeans with worn thighs, along with a pair of shoes and socks. These she arranged outside, first on the decking, then in the meadow grass, finally tossing them over the lower branches of a juniper tree. At each position she took several photographs.

For some shots it was as if a person had stripped hastily. Why would they do that? Bunched jeans and kicked away shoes. Another arrangement involved careful folding – the clothes became a kind of origami, depicting geometric shapes in parallel, in degrees of closeness.

Sarah stalked around her site. In her new post-queasy body she felt frail. It cloaked her like an aura. Something was misaligned in the photos. The clothes were like crumpled ghosts, or not even that, like sheets cast off by ghosts whose souls had disintegrated. Those gun smugglers from the bus. Lights in the bus station and the way they had walked off, been led off. Cold roads and sirens. Long guns carried upright. Empty poses in a post-apocalyptic world. Didn't America always lend itself to that, to twig and abandoned wrapping and vast sky. A small neat cabin is the only comfort. Her vague immigrant thoughts disintegrated.

Grass blade.

Foldings.

Vast.

And the moon rose.

A galleon.

This city can make you feel brand new.

Collar.

Black coffee.

Spilled a little from the spoon when I stirred.

Grass blades against the shirt – adjust –

If there were any emotions involved they were clear threads within the whole parcel of visions and ritualised movements. Hard to pick out. Possibly parasitic worms.

Sarah passed herself over the margin of field and wood. Intuitive art. Bodily fluids should be involved. Spilt substance. Milk, or blood. Sarah reached a hand to her weighty breast. It hung against the palm. It didn't even feel empty. Blood then. She fingered the Swiss Army knife in her pocket. Determining whether to spread herself around a little. The repulsion and ecstasy of a disrupted body. She flicked open the blade with her left hand and looked at the palm of her right. There was the scar. She opened and closed her hand. Pushed the tip of the knife along the edge of the scar. Just lightly. As if cutting into a peach the biting metal was fluid against the tenderness. She stopped and knelt down. A very thin line of blood ran down into the grass. Overhead a murmuration of small birds banked in the sky, though the sun was still high and the wind in the pines was not the evening wind which she was familiar with now. And her upward palm was still holding nothing.

Her phone was buzzing. She breathed out. Then, in her best BBC voice, 'Hello, Sarah Browne speaking.'

'Hey, it's me, Theo. Calling to apologise.'

'Oh, that's fine, that's fine,' said Sarah, 'for leaving this morning, was it?'

'Yeah, I'm sorry,' he said, 'I'm coming over, right? Sarah?'

'Please do,' she pressed end. Scrunched her lips. He was coming to check she wasn't pregnant with his mediocre sex baby.

Sarah went inside and opened a fresh aspirin blister with her thumbnail and filled a glass and it was all down her tilted throat in one go. Blood on the glass. Then she had to sit down: Everything still ached, good. She drew in sighs and the cabin was soundless and intact but only for a few minutes more. This was all a performance piece, wasn't it.

She put the pocket knife on the coffee table stained blade out, surrounded by little droplets that would melt into the wood. Dear émigré with your wooden walls around you. How long can you calmly sit putting this gutty collage together sticking the bits back on when they fall off, before it sits up and looks right at you. And you acknowledge this other, American you. Sombre. Monstrous, many, one.

Wasn't it art though, wasn't it better than what she had ever attempted before.

Theo knocked at the door. She let him in with the clear sunlight before shutting it crisply out. Despite the large front windows, the cabin at that hour was dim. She smiled to be welcoming. She wished she had cigarettes. Something to bite between her teeth.

'Sarah, hey, you all right?' Theo asked, 'Gam said you were sick or something, and she had to take you to the pharmacy?'

He held a parcel under his arm and despite his words of concern seemed to be enjoying this melodrama, poised and full of tender suspicion. Sarah continued to smile.

'Yes, yes. I am now, anyway. Bad times. And I told Gam it was food poisoning.'

'Oh,' then, 'that sucks.' He walked over to the kitchenette and put his parcel down. Sarah searched his eyes, but it was dim back in there too.

'Tea?' she asked. A good thing, perhaps, that Theo couldn't hear the subtle fuck you of the offer. There is a certain nearly overt movement you can make. The one that marked the breaking of strings, or of the finest hairs. All she had to do was turn herself with sharpness, once, and let the many ends be severed from one another.

'Now,' she said, pouring water in the kettle, 'what's in the parcel?'

'Yeah, I had something for you,' Theo said, 'let me—'

And he held the small blank package out to her. Sarah grazed his fingertips with hers when taking it, left handed. Hoping it added to his old-fashioned, manly discomfort.

She tore down one fold and something heavy shifted down to the bottom. She peered inside. The package contained a white envelope and a small bag made of artisan paper inside of which was a shape carved out of a single piece of banded wood.

She carefully took it out to avoid bloodstains. It was an animal with a long, undulating tail notched with stars, a small plump body, a snout, smooth ears. A wooden squirrel.

'There's a town to the east where they make 'em. I got it a while ago, before the spring. Realised today I was hanging on to it for you.'

'Thank you,' Sarah rubbed her thumb down the tail. It felt good, like impacted sand. 'I like how you think that line will work on me.'

'In a way it's true,' Theo said, coming close, rubbing the wooden creature also, but not leaning his head against hers, but touching her thumb with his, in a tender, temporary way.

'What happened to your hand?'

Sarah exchanged the gift for her cup of tea on the counter.

'I'll open the envelope later.'

The creature sat looking out at the room. It couldn't be called kitsch or childish. It possessed a readable, faintly benevolent, character.

'So,' Theo said, with a sigh, 'I guess the next thing we have to talk about is about my mother's weed growing and delivery business.'

'Oh God, yes,' Sarah had forgotten and hid her mouth, smirking.

'You laugh, it pisses me off,' Theo said. 'She sells it mostly to the Sunflower Retreat women, over on yellow mesa. She's smart, but—'

'Sunflower Retreat? Is that like a cult?' She drank more tea and felt that everything was about drinking tea, and touching inanimate objects and being ever so pleasant.

'No, a commune. Started in the seventies I think. All-women, making arts and crafts, selling produce. They gave her those chickens and materials for the coop as payment one time.'

'So you're not running any big drug deals down on the streets of Esta then?'

'She knows the police would take one look at me, my

surname, and ffft, locked up.'

'Because you're Hispanic, right?'

'Uh, yeah. Probably deport me to Mexico.'

'They'd do that? I take it you've never lived in Mexico.'

Theo shook his head. 'Everyone, my grandmothers, mother, father, were born within two dozen miles of here. Spoke Spanish at home, with the Castilian lisp, the way people round the Valles Caldera do, but American as,' he hesitated, 'as all that. But all that counts for shit. If you look like this and speak Spanish beyond fourth grade level,' he paused, holding up his hands, 'fuck it.'

'The immensity of the subject of Mexican-Americans or Hispanic-Americans, or Chicanos, whatever they get called cannot be conveyed to your satisfaction or my enlightenment in one conversation?' Sarah looked at him over her cup.

'Yeah, that's it. You could read up on this stuff. I'll lend you *Borderlands/La Frontera*; *The New Mestiza*. Gloria Anzaldúa. She explains it well, at least get you started there.'

'You read a lot of theory in your spare time?'

'I worked in a library, certain books caught my eye.'

'Did you steal them?'

Theo shrugged. 'I will get my way to the words that matter.'

'Fighting the system, I see,' she said.

Sunlight had shifted outside and a sudden spot of light created a golden shield, high up on the front wall, highlighting part of a painting of a waterfall that Sarah had put up. The painting's greys and scratches, glowing silver. Theo murmured something.

'What?' she asked.

'Nothing. I just said, pretty. You have to pay attention to the little things.'

'I suppose,' Sarah said, 'if you want to start that.' She sat on the arm of the sofa, and put her hand on her face, smoothening the skin. Theo came over and rubbed her arm until she stopped disliking him quite so much.

'Let's go outside, I need some air,' she said.

The high desert air was comparable to no other thing. Sarah took slow, fevered breaths of it.

'So, where next?' said Theo. 'I mean, if you aren't too sick, you want to head up north a little? I know a town that saw some trouble – kind of half a ghost town. Also this fort not far from there. I found it myself, thought it was cool.'

Sarah listened to the valley's insects a moment before she answered.

'Sounds my thing,' she said. 'Ghost towns, forts, ruins and shit.' She looked at him, smiling precisely. The dislike had swung back again. Something to do with the way he was walking on the great edgeless lawn like nothing was failing, as if he could be talking to anyone. She had an urge to have her Swiss Army knife in hand again and to raise the blade at him and pace towards him everything glittering drama everything promising rapturous breach.

Theo smiled back. Cute Sarah, cute phrases. She was sure her eyes must say something interior and vicious, but probably they didn't even look ill. When you are sly you give up your transparencies, even if you crave them sometimes.

She let herself grow cool. Ahead the blackish wood cabin, the swoop of the Valle Grande was all around, and the caldera sides all rugged and pined. The faint sky above was painted on. Below, two small figures stood agreeing on a time of departure to the ruins. Neither was moving in an agitated way. They parted the way lovers should, with a little fine salting of regret, but not too much.

61

Night pressed down hard on the Valle, shut down the profiles of trees and left them formless, restless. Sarah thought about silence: it never seemed possible until it moved in like a huge river of ice. Flickers of silence were not enough to appreciate the magnitude. At first encounter a true, frozen noiselessness hems you, then your thoughts rebel and multiply.

Sarah had kept Theo's letter pristine. She sat on the floor with the waiting envelope inches from her socked feet, while she drank down a box of merlot she'd bought from the liquor store in Esta a few days before. Tight-lipped puckery pulls to get the liquid down without it scouring too much. The wine burned like a urinary tract infection. Liquor store box wine, it was a beautiful phrase: American in a way she could get behind. Foreign-familiar. It had cost four dollars for two litres and she was going to demolish it.

Even bad wine puts everything into soft focus.

She pictured Theo frightened, but concealing it, leaning faux-casual against the kitchen surface, his neck held stiff, crisp collar to his shirt. She pictured a shadow across his brow, lighting like a Hollywood monochrome, long shadows and the dramatic music. Someone behind the camera adjusts the focus. Another, dishevelled with feeling, examines the script to find where it all fits, the livid precision needed to choreograph the moment.

Perhaps if she could think of any damn thing without the intrusion of this obsession with unreality. She got up clumsily and lit the fire before it became impossible to do so. What if there was a cheque in the envelope for an abortion? How to feel about that. Great, money. Her womb anyway was plugged inside with a metallic spike. Popped up in her while in London.

Punk IUD, she liked to think.

Sarah got up and fetched a bread knife, for ceremony. She sliced open the envelope and unfolded the letter – white as apple flesh. It was printed on soft, high rag paper. She supposed his actual writing would be rounded and badly spaced from lack of daily use, like nearly everybody's, but the words were typewritten, uneven on the page. There was a high chance he had used a vintage typewriter.

The letter was pretty, the letter was long and poorly edited. It contained several declarations of love and devotion. These were masked in irony, and later, doleful insistence that Sarah, poor girl, could not feel romantic impulses, that she was a bitch to Gam and unforgiving on the whole. But that Theo, really, could see beyond all that. It talked only obliquely about what to do about 'the scare'. The letter was signed 'with truth and authenticity'.

Sarah pursed her lips until she felt them whiten and dry. She looked at the paper, how the niceness of it had been ruined. She wiped her fire-warmed forehead on a corner of her robe. It was a kimono-sleeved affair, Madonna blue. Up close the pattern was blurred into something, like lace thrown into long blue grass. She sometimes felt weird in Japanese-style things. As if trying too hard to reach across the void. Whatever. It was good to have pretty things. Pretty things are stable and will never let you down. A joy forever. She felt drunk. She calmly folded the letter neatly back into the envelope, and then into the folds of the fire. What still holds true is that love letters burn so well.

62

Sarah had a box of salt. She had her boots – yes. One boot right foot, one boot left foot. On the salt packaging there was a little dainty girl with a yellow umbrella, like something you would see tattooed on a bartender. Sarah pulled on her wool coat. Okay, let's be against forgiveness, nicety. Fuck lots, the lot. Let's walk out in the night and wreck something.

The door closed loudly behind her. Sarah scuffed forward in her winter boots. She felt classy in them. Underneath the coat, she wore pyjamas. She stumbled a little and dropped the salt, but caught it again, no harm done.

Up the dry road she walked, glad of the cold. Making her clever again as she crossed into Coronado territory. No Theo on guard at the window or on the roof. Asleep. Gam too, because Sarah couldn't hear the TV – it was late, of course. It was, wasn't it? Sarah turned her wrist to look at her watch that wasn't there. There was no tick tick. No time, no bomb.

Dead grass and gravel crunched. She thought of cereal back in London at eighteen, corn flakes and milk had been all she had eaten, reasoning they were cheap, healthy with their list of vitamins, and that she could strike a pose while eating them. She would focus on the phrase on the box, 'ice cold milk' to make it more luxurious. Slow spoonfuls, trying to get every bit of taste out of the over-familiar. And the texture of them becoming like little dry lizard tongues she cracked against her teeth. When she got back to the cabin she would try to eat something but probably it wouldn't work.

Sneak. Wine-headed. Salt under her arm like a talisman. What's the salt for? Silly questions. Salt purifies and it poisons. What better use could she put it to – and there already was the greenhouse, like a dirty green-white cake on a shelf, in amongst the saplings.

She could smell raked grass clippings, amplified by the dark. And though she had hoped to feel immediate all night long, there she had instead the fields behind the Warne, playing snake-in-the-grass with some other kids, their names long forgotten. The twins. The boy with one blue eye and one brown, rock-thrower like a giant, all the way down splosh into the creek. The double-jointed girl who would hide in the cleverest places. With Sarah, if they were friends that day.

Sarah yanked the greenhouse door until it was the slightest ajar and slid herself in through the gap. She bristled at the hot wet air, walking in, trailing her palms over the glass and support beams for the light switch. She really should know better. Keep it off. So rarely there is a dark like this in the world. A sea of dark, rich and perfumed. Dark made her shapeless, negating what she was doing. God is the dark.

Sarah went down the rows towards the far end. She bumped her knee against the desk and cast her phone across it. In the top drawer there was an open cardboard box containing many smaller packets – she tilted it and reached in. Rolling papers. She took out and pocketed a pair of silver scissors and after a brief pause a packet of rollers and a pre-stuffed baggie because you have to, really.

The plan was: start at the back where she was, and work her way down to the door then leave.

She turned and crouched in the central aisle at the foot of the nearest plant, and hacked the scissors into the potting earth, cutting some of the larger roots. Then she raised the container of salt and pulled out the little spout. It sounded soothing. Once there was sufficient salt, Sarah covered the roots back over with soil, and wiped the lower, dirtied stems clean.

The fanless air was like sandwich film across her face. As she worked, she grew calm and less drunk. This was a good plan. Theo would be unburdened but probably really angry with her. A good fight with fierce, wall-shaking make-up sex afterwards. She presumed anyway. She'd work on the seduction part later, she was good at that. Once Gam twigged about the salting she would be agonised and bitter but who would she tell? Her friends at the commune, now devoid of their weed. Oh them. She imagined sympathetic nods, burst cushions, patchouli fog. Say their fingerpaint canvases discarded on a dusty table. Or their woolfelt succulents half-stitched. All these women, decrying her in soft tones. That, to her, was triumph on all fronts.

When Sarah was at last done, the night was beginning to lift, a shard of orange-yellow sliced through the trees like pure glory. She made for home. Her actions fell away and became historic.

63

Sarah piled clothes on the bed and began raking through them for the warmest and least ugly. She climbed into her bed again and looked at the time: 5:45am. She was passably sober but maybe Theo should drive for the first hour. Now there was nothing to do but stare and occupy that state between after-drunk and hung-over until she didn't have enough time to get ready.

Lying there, off-kilter, Sarah thought of the greenhouse, how the salt was sucking the moisture out of the roots and secretly withering the whole. She smiled, or she made an attempt, it was too early to move her face correctly. She rubbed her temples and thought of how it might be awful later, travelling with Theo.

She imagined repeating the salt dose on a wider scale. The rainforests first. Start with the largest, then on to the beech woods and oak, the redwoods, the mixed birch forests of the taiga. A thick residue of salt left to cake the felled skeletons of all those beautiful old trees. Their trunks would be impervious to decay since the bacteria and fungi and beetles were all dead and mummified too. Imagine the deserts of Brazil, the slimy salt pits of the Pacific Northwest. Would she do that? Yes. If it were possible and she had infinite time and no one asked her what she was doing. She would kill and make perfect.

Sarah held her head up with her elbow on the windowsill, quiet and smiling. She looked out for a cool length of time. The wood under her elbow was smooth and dry, the heart cords marked in it were blackly puckered and each one known to her. Her hair straight and long spilt into her lap. She was regal, a queen in posture, all it took was a deliberate deadening of anything outside the senses, and a concomitant magnification of those.

This is all of it a performance. Sarah, years eighteen to twenty-seven. If she could only draw herself now, make a tapestry of herself as she was at that moment. Full of grog-muddied blood. The delicacy of the dawn lifting the skirts of things. And her quilted blanket and untouched, fine-haired limbs.

Who has time for guilt, but to side-eye it as it passes.

What she would spend her money on

Counselling. No, listen. She'd pay an immobile gentleman or lady a fat sum to say, I'm sensing some hostility, or whatever it was they would say unto the harpy Sarah beating her green-black wings against the bookshelves and shrieking. Shrieking about something inhuman and full like a black flock of all-denied majesty. Pearls at her throat and a dress also of feathers and a borderline personality level of neckline. That's what they'd do, they'd pathologise her fashion choices and keep their silence on her gore-stained teeth. She'd pay her money to be told she was not a monster nothing of the like but something quite domestic who should adjust itself to the world, for better peace of mind.

Sarah with her money would levitate, incredible wingspan, bluster from them beating the books from the shelves the notes scattered. And she would shriek again and crash through the window of the office – they always had floor to ceiling windows, for such moments – and in a rain of glass she would escape and be always magnificent monstrous female spurious and headed on to the next city to sack.

64

Where the broad caldera folded a crook in the mountains, Sarah and Theo stopped to let a herd of elk pass by. Huge brown bulwarks with the elegance of a flotilla of galleons, clumbering up the slope and over the culvert. Twenty or thirty of them near, and countless more puddling on the grassland. And others already crossed into the lower hills among the trembling aspens. They had great thick necks and peaceful eyes, and their muzzles reminded Sarah of camels; rounded drooping mouths that seemed to express some low inner sorrow. Mouths like the hands of the elderly covered in felt socks.

'A group of females,' said Theo, whispering.

'Do you recognise any of them?'

Theo leaned forward.

'Uh, like two or three of them,' he said at last, 'I'm not that good yet. They have been tagged, maybe by me, maybe by some of the calving season guys.'

After a time the ones who were crossing had crossed, leaving their more cautious sisters stranded on the valley side. Theo put on the handbrake, waiting them out.

'So,' Sarah said, watching the beasts plodding uphill as if immersed in some thicker element than air, 'the elk cross the road and we sit, and there is supposed to be some epiphany.'

Theo breathed out slowly.

'Uh. Guess I could tell you about the difference between an elk and a moose?'

'Go on then.'

He spoke on the subject. Sarah listened more for tone. She found it hard to keep a grip on the smooth, enthusiastic voice. He belonged out there with them, hunting them weaponless from the tree cover. Or living with them. A silent, observational life: he might be a good man then. Worthwhile in his quirks.

His day would include making a morning pilgrimage to the herd. Trailing them in the woods. In wintertime, they would head south over the yellow rocks and the red down into the Bandelier pasture. Not that she fucking knew where they went for winter. She could really see him. Elk skins on his back. Elk skin boots. Putting his hand in their mouths and holding it there and whispering to them. Not aroused but not inert either.

'You can't touch the antlers when they're in velvet,' said Theo, 'it hurts them. They are delicate until the blood supply cuts and it rubs off.'

Sarah slumped into her chair. The beast nearest the car ticked its ear and raised one foot, put it down again.

65

They made it to Española with no broaching of Theo's love letter. Española, a town, Theo said offhand, whose heart had stopped beating when the railroad ebbed. It was mundane now, constructed of a webbing of multiple crossroads and gum-coloured fast food places. The local restaurants had Mexican detailing and Sarah found them painfully sad. Though why she did not know. She was feeling hung-over and the green rivers of Chama and Grande flashed insistently under a red and rising sun.

Back before anything Anglo had been built, this area had been declared capital of the New World for the glory of Spain. That was anno domini 1598. Here at that time nothing but open scrubland and a people of the adobe townships – Pueblo peoples, descendants of Bandelier – for our friends the conquistadors to murder.

The road took them out of Española and bracketed all its histories and effacement. That was the truth about roads. They remove you. They shear you down to a fine point of light and keep you going, clean of blame.

There was silence in the car but Sarah couldn't tell of what kind. They switched sides by a lake that shone like a salt flat. Sarah drove them northwards, all the time hoping that something would change, would be kind to look at. But the landscape only blurred from dust to bushland, unstoried.

They passed a place whose name meant "Onion" in Spanish. Theo told her, before he nodded his head to his chest and fell asleep.

Nothing for a long while.

A pale belly of land. And in Sarah a weightless weight and an unshifting non-sickness, boredom, unease, hip-deep sexual frustration, one or more of those.

Then a sign that said "Los Ojos" twenty miles. She had heard it somewhere, seen it written. "The eyes", wasn't it?

Eyes on a playing card.

Eyes on the side of a boat.

She felt the name bundle and push at her. With pupils swivelling.

Eyes from a book, from a movie. Cat's eyes, elk eyes, devil's eyes.

Eyes in the mirror that looked dully back. Bloodshot eye. Spotlight eyes searching. She tugged at her shirt sleeves as if covering her wrists would fix her. Sarah was shivering. And her own eyes were sick of the nothing scrolling on intolerably forever with no fucking point to it, not even a single goddamn tree.

Down off to the left she could just about see a tide of low evergreens washing around promontories of pink fleshy sandstone. Pinkish dust under her feet and rocks like broken pottery. Something a mile or two away glittered black, a lake or a stretch of abandoned concrete paving. The sun on her neck like a reminder. You could howl and no one would know. Okay, Theo, theoretically. That's all he was, theoretical. In every situation he was a flimsy line sketch. All the wrong angles and charcoal dust. That was one thing that was fixable. She pulled out her phone.

'Hello, Gam? Georgiana?' Sarah spoke quietly because the desert dust carried little harms that nicked her eyes. 'It's me, listen.'

Listen. I will tell of my wickedness. How I broke in and salted everything.

Listen. Reduce me to the present tense. Hate me and make your boy hate me later. Make me the baddy. Just make something fucking happen.

Clap your hands and we'll all believe, for the moment, in catharsis.

Tierra Amarilla was an arrow right. The low hills surrounding the turnoff were black with ponderosa and juniper. At least, Sarah always guessed those two. She had looked up more names of pines, but those were the most evocative, so those were what they were. Theo was curled up in the passenger seat. When Sarah turned off the engine he stirred.

'I fell asleep?' He said, stretching, 'Uuh, we're here. Cool. First off, look at this.'

He pointed across to a roadside marker, the kind Sarah had seen before at spots of interest. She got out. This one was far more weathered than any of the others. Certain lines had been scratched out. Scratched over many times in a way that was most certainly deliberate.

'What is this?' Sarah asked, reading, 'land rights... government troops...'

'What I can tell, it's about a disagreement between the state and Chicano claimants to the land. There was some trouble here in the sixties. You'll see when we get down there.' Theo rubbed his right cheekbone, and smiled a little with his eyes closed, full of sand.

They steered off the highway and into the town.

It was eerily still. No foot traffic and no shops. Several shuttered houses with grass sniping through the windows. There wasn't a Walmart either, not for miles, so that wasn't what had drained the town. Sarah got out her camera and lowered the windows. She drew up next to a boarded up building with the faded lettering, saloon, and a balcony above. Where of an evening the whores might have leaned fanning themselves and calling and cackled down. It was so quiet that Sarah could hear the creak of the exposed stairs. On the saloon's crooked half-door a flannel shirt had been left to bleach and crumble.

She might have been a whore, coming out here. Or she'd have worked the piano, badly, being a sight too sharp-toothed for other business. But didn't you want your hotel, your garden with peach trees? Didn't you want soil in the ruts of your palm? You must choose. Self-sufficiency or silk skirts raised above your squirming lap or grinning for the drunk men tap the ivory sing badly, bottles against your temple. But none seem an option when you have your own peripheral existence, a salt chaos, when you try to say calm, poise, but you understand break, blood, founder.

They rolled on down Main.

'I don't like this,' said Sarah, tasting salt, flecks of old plastic.

'It's pretty weird, right?'

'I'm going to turn around, so I can get a better angle.'

Many dead homes with windows boarded. And in some these boards removed and the glass behind knocked out. Sarah imagining she heard the faint ominous clicks of the Geiger each time they slowed.

68

The road out of Tierra Amarilla took them across scrubby fields with neither cattle nor crops in them. On through a heathland reminiscent of land edging a sea, but there was no sea. A billboard advertised an artificial freshwater fishing lake. Under the headlines and boasts was a drawing in a crude, nineteen-sixties style of a large green salmon-like creature, flopping, with a grin on its face, into the net of a fisherman. The fisherman also had a grin and was clamping his hand to his hat to keep it from flying off out of pure glee into a cloudless sky.

There was no one on this road.

Once though, Sarah looked through the dirt on the windscreen and saw a police car parked on a parallel road, nose towards them, motionless.

Sarah concentrated on driving until the boredom itched too much. She looked at Theo slapping his hand lazily, cocky, against the flank of the car. Another wave of disgust. The car veered right. Ahead was the reservoir from the billboard. Lake of bright dead blue, under the blue above and rimmed with silver sandbanks like scimitars.

A car park for the reservoir was next to a field pitted with prairie dog burrows and Sarah had the odd sensation of dozens of tiny heads watching her, disappearing and re-emerging. On the far side of the lake parched, unlovely hills stood high enough to obscure hope of a view.

She could remember having seen a horror film that took place somewhere quite like this. Her mouth still tasted plastic. She took her coat out from the boot, put it on, and zipped it up to her mouth.

'We're planning on camping here, are we?'

'Huh, doesn't look open,' said Theo. 'Guess I'll check

though.'

He walked off to a sign standing by a boarded ranger station, then strolled back. The whole time, little heads rhythmically bobbed up and down to look at him. Prairie dogs have language; they can describe an individual human by their height build the colour of their jacket, all in a burst of a bark half a second long. Brrirreeek. Sarah felt a sneering laugh stifle at the back of her throat. Brrirreek; lost travellers idiotic no danger reported.

Left to herself for a while she went over to the high bank and looked down. Under the lake it was obvious there was an ancient hidden town. Smoke from fires furled up on still nights and lured the campers from the land into the water, where they forgot themselves, and the surface rose above them in mercury colours. Animals ate the bodies when they washed to shore.

Theo strode over.

'Yup, sign says closed,' he said. 'You wanna pitch the tent anyway?'

'No.'

'Oh? Why not?'

'Well, because, if you hadn't noticed, it's creepy as fuck out here.'

'Creepy,' said Theo, swiping at dust on the windscreen. Moving dust from his hand onto his jeans. 'Creepy as fuck. When did you get so chicken? Let's go to the fort, and then you say to me this, this is creepy.'

Sarah watched him walk away. Chicken? Like something a thirteen-year-old-kid would say in an eighties movie. She walked back to the car with tight movements. Something shrill in the back of her head. Whatever. Just keep going to the end of the day, then sleep. The world is always being ominous. Ominous or bitter. Sarah glanced about for something to bash her elbow against, to shift this clingy feeling and do it subtly. But there was nothing but her car, the brilliant air, and the high bank of the man-made, man-eating lake.

She tucked her hair behind her ears, aware of a panic surge tickling her chest. Beside her Theo was irritated. He was a blank-faced mannequin in the passenger seat. How easily he could lean over and grab her by the neck and smash her head repeatedly on the wheel. Sarah held her breath a long time and when she breathed out her nostrils burned. She touched her face and it was covered in a film of dirt and salt and something moist.

'So, where's the turn for the fort?' she asked.

'All right, we're doing this?'

'Yep. For posterity,' she answered.

Theo shifted to look at her.

'Shit. How are you doing, Sarah?'

Sarah said nothing

'Later, or tell me, whenever,' Theo said. 'Let's have a look around first. I guess. Since we're here. It's really cool.'

Then this was just about the letter. He was so petty, prim, lean, sour. A collection of descriptors under a pleasant skin. And how else to be, when he couldn't see the flares or hear the frantic clicks emanating from her person. A dull siren starting up at her temple. She opened her mouth.

'Sure. Later. Sure.'

She wanted to come and stand in the wreckage.

Of all the things Sarah could hope for, it was this: that she would step gingerly about a cleanly broken place. Old blood and shadows seen lying thick on the ground, and the feeling of being unharried. Mentally turn the bones up to the light like an archaeologist. Bring what cold logic she could. See the relics, old signs, chipped cups, what have you, as between human and nothing human any longer. To discover solidified time and not to feel unstable and vicious as she did right then, in the absence of graspable fact and at the mercy of her violent mind.

She parked at the gateway to the ruined fort. It looked like rugby or American football goal posts, composed of two long poles and a banner of crackled, faded yellow at the top where the name had been painted once in the colours of the New Mexican sun-flag. The only barrier was a small red and white striped blockade at the base that they could easily step around, and did.

They walked under a dark overgrowth of deciduous trees. Warped from winds and neglect. Below their feet were impacted little rocks mixed with weeds and stamped here and there by pawed, pronged feet.

Theo was talking more than usual. Sarah silent. The content of Theo's speech was not important. The importance was in their bodies pushing on uphill. The importance was always in getting the body through this with mastery and graceful artifice.

Nothing could ever change about this place. Beside the white road was a squat green hut with shattered windows on three sides. A checkpoint station. Inside was space for a chair, a desk, and a little shelf. The shelf remained. It was where the entry log must have sat, prim and filled with faithful detail. A puzzle of leaves and rusted things comforted and confused underfoot. The walls gaped, swollen, bleached. Sarah touched things with the tips of her fingers, testing and hoping for a splinter or just the right tiny cut. Theo was dumb as old brickwork beside her.

A house crouched further uphill and inside, a set of old-fashioned ovens, stamped with KEWANEE PORTABLE FIREBOX BOILER. Scraps of metal knotted on the floor under impossibly thin broken panes of glass. They had been knocked out of the high windows. Cracked like that cashier's gum when Sarah stepped on them. Sarah smelled the air for charred notes, but the only odour was of a dry must, and the sweat off their tense bodies.

'So, what you think of all this?' called Theo.

'Yes,' she answered, with awe in her voice, like a gift.

71

Aunt Selene in the library with the bottle of '78 Porto, teeth purpled. Hair up in a harsh bun held with an ancient hairpin of waxy flowers and nails long and yellow scratching the rim of her glass. Queen of the ten habitable rooms of the Warne. A picture of how best to terrify a thirteen-year-old. Lucy out. Mum out. No one to overhear, to contradict, to speak out for what was just.

'I told her to get rid of you, you know,' Aunt Selene had said, 'when we found out, Maud basically stuck a straw in a bottle of vodka. We thought you'd turn out delayed. And we had our hands full with Lucy. So I tried to convince her she'd be much better off getting you hoovered up.'

Her words sounded very practised, though that was probably because adult Sarah had thought them so many times. Though at the time she'd just thought urgh. The thing about girlhood is you are so often misunderstood by enemies who are older than you. They tend to think you are fitted with basic stuff like respect – that is, fear – of your elders. That you will be open and tender and will react in the ways they anticipate to their fists crushing you. Usually they have no idea what they are doing, in Sarah's experience. They do not know humans at all, so they practice on teenagers and expect they will win. And all that without knowing what victories they are after.

Sarah had sat on the small leather stool, poking through a magazine nearly as old as the port.

'I wouldn't have cared if she had, would I?'

'You turned out such a sweet girl too,' said Selene not acknowledging Sarah's response, 'aren't I glad she didn't listen?'

And Sarah, being indestructible and worse than Selene could reckon, had got up nonchalantly and headed to the doorway, as if to get herself something from the kitchen. Then turned on her heels, to linger—

'Mum told me about your husband. I'm sorry. I'm so sorry,' she said. Because the best way to be hurtful is to sound kind, she had learned that in that house. 'Did you find the body? Or was it Mum? I wonder what you could have said to him for him to go and do that.'

'You little cunt. Get out. And go fuck yourself!' Aunt Selene had shouted, 'fuck you!' Aunt Selene glasses deep in a blood-red sea of port, 'you miserable bastard cunt!' Aunt Selene, grey dress and death at her throat and eyes like a wounded thing that did not even know it was.

'Well, whichever. See you later Aunt Selene, try not to fall in the fire and die.' Sarah delivered a good smirk, and turned away with a quick curtsey.

Glass shatters with a pleasant fullness of sound against a heavy oak frame. It feels good and terrible like you are getting away with something, as it echoes, as you run over the flagstones of the empty corridor, lightly on the soles of your feet, shaken and rotten to your core.

72

Sarah peered down a long turquoise hall to read the graffiti DO NOT ENTER done in red spray. Theo was talking again and moving in an agitated manner. Sarah looked away at a blinding desert sky over neat rolling hills. Hills like England, if too dry. Far too dry. Love letters burn so well. Everything else could burn too, so why not.

Theo took off towards the flank of a long hall. Sarah followed. Through the broken façade she saw up on the first floor a tiled room. Five smaller inconsolable box rooms later, the same tiled room repeated. The bathroom, for a corridor of men who had once bunked in rooms now gutted like bellies, hung to dry. A barracks or mess or whatever it was called. Facilities for some long gone army. The place had texture. Ceiling tiles dangled, parts of the wall were torn up. Speckles of graceful light marked out wire, trash, grimy panelling. More graffiti at the other entrance read NATAS, next to a pentagram. COLD WAR GHOSTS? beside a frail-looking phantom. Shotgun shells lay scattered, blasts out of the plaster. Shotgun shells looked like chemist shop lipbalm casings. Cherries, she tasted fake cherry flavour and rubbed her lips together. It made sense that this place was a hangout for local kids. If she had grown up around here, it would have called to her.

Bottles of vodka and passing round cigarettes. Or painting their thumbnails with a new design. Roses, glitter, waves. Black and purple, silver and red stripes. They would have had eyes that glowed in the dark, children of the aftermath. Or they'd pretend to. Kicking dust about and watching the sun rise between beery fingers. Is that Venus, that star? How the fuck should I know. Got to get back before my mom and dad find out. Got to get back in time to get breakfast and to get ready for school.

Sarah immersed herself, merging herself with this reality. As if it was not alien. As if she could be at home here ever. She called to Theo, 'Did you come here when you were younger?'

'Huh—'

He twisted round and his foot caught against a hunk of masonry. He fell hard, and there was the sound of glass cracking. How had he managed that? He held up his hands at his terrible relationship with gravity.

'Goddamn glass is everywhere.'

'Did any stick you?' Sarah asked.

'No,' he said, not looking at her, 'no. Seems I fall a lot when you're around. But I don't know if that means anything.'

'Don't breathe, that's asbestos you're on,' Sarah said, 'that yellow fluff. Or I think so. As a precaution you shouldn't breathe. Or speak too much.' She stood back. 'How far is the nearest hospital, just out of interest?'

'Too far,' said Theo, gently picking grit out of a bloody scuff on his shin through a rip in his jeans. 'I'll live. Look, Sarah, don't you have anything to say at all? About all this, everything.' The scuff began to bleed brightly. Sarah smiled, meek or cruel, whichever.

'Yes, I have, of course.'

And then said nothing else. And clicked her tongue and shrugged, walking off amid the ruins.

73

She felt Theo a good distance behind to her left, a crouched dark shape.

Why am I so terrible, why have I always been so terrible, she thought in a flat way. There was a peculiar smell like paint, other respiratory hazards. The moon was visible. When you see both the moon and the sun in the sky at once it is an omen if you want it to be. To her left she thought she saw the lake of the dead. Her shadow reached across an empty lawn, a clawed elongated monster. It was impossible to change course. Theo should stop trying. She wanted to hurt him terribly. And the earth should go out like a light for mercy.

The harshest things are so simple to say. Despite this being so, not everyone deserves the worst. But who is not everyone. Distinguishing between people seemed a terrible burden. With nothing else to do but wait for the end, Sarah waited, quite calm on the surface. But underneath, under the calm she told herself, she was slowly disintegrating into a terrible void a maelstrom a din of music that she could taste in plastic and heat and something metallic. But she was pretty in her clothes and her movements were almost easy, out of all that practice.

A late afternoon wind got going in a school of saplings clustered in the foundations of a roofless prefab. Hissing down the turquoise hallways, it touched at the old discarded nails, rolled them for a game. Blew the dust about on the floor. Just as had the first gust to find an open door and no one to stop it.

Theo said, 'Guess coming here was a mistake.'

'Yeah, maybe,' Sarah called back.

Theo's profile had shrunk. He was still crouched on the ground. He tied a shoelace in slow motion, stood with equal deliberate slowness. Sarah squinted at the sky for a moment again, cleared her throat.

'Maybe it's just too much. Too abandoned.'

'"The notion of emptiness generates passion",' Theo answered, standing, 'Theodore Roethke.'

'Are you sure? Sounds like Samuel Beckett.'

Theo wrinkled his nose.

'I'm sure. I'm a Theodore myself.'

'Is that true?'

'Yeah. So, what he means, I think, is that it's the notion, not the emptiness itself, that's real.'

'The notion, the acting of the notion.'

'Maybe there isn't any empty thing. It's just you have the idea it's empty. It's kinda like a loud, distorting fiction that distracts you and makes it all too fucking difficult.'

'Yep. Living my life like that, one hundred per cent,' Sarah said. Theo laughed. It was a sad laugh, but he didn't know, poor fucker. In spite of it all the afternoon broke, became evening.

74

They walked back down to the car, Theo limping and Sarah at a pace behind, letting him limp.

She was overburdened with her thoughts. A wish for comfort, for palm against palm and fingers latched. No one ever knew how to give her it. What could she want, given that she seemed to everyone a pretty cactus or a thistle pitched all by itself among the rocks, casting a twisted shadow. She had read parables, she knew even God didn't want a wretch. Not even the best or worst girls of literature could talk her down. She was no one's project. She walked around a rut of leaves and insulation, but registering with a kind of pride the chilling air, her feet hitting and rising from the ground with a nice definitiveness. The car in front. Dulling footless miles ahead. Only night, moonless or unmooned, could swallow her whole, she thought. Her hope was to at least catch in its throat.

'I was thinking, actually we might want to set up the tent. It's going to be dark, what, in the next hour…' she said.

'Fine. If you want to be here.'

'Just, we're sort of running out of options. I don't fancy driving back all that way in the dark.'

'Fine. Sure.'

Sarah looked down at her shadow, now less sinister, and wondered if it ever wearied of her. If it did in fact slide off when the dark fell.

They returned with the necessary materials and chose a flattish area halfway up the hill. They knelt to undo packs and thread metal-tipped bones through the tent skin. They stood to prop it all up then kicked the guy hooks in with the heels of their boots. The soil was loamy and without stones. Sarah thought of the ocean long withdrawn, a land deprived of the grace of the sea.

They got inside the tent. Blue sterility.

They sat cross-legged with their eyes turned away. Sarah thought of cherries and gunshots. Theo thought of whatever. Their breath clung to their solitary lips. And what then? A rush of awkwardness wending through the pores like old stitches. Cut offs of speech. Hands picking out books. The gas canister held up for evaluation, utility. Hiss. Sarah opened the zipper and put the stove outside and heated a saucepan of water for tea.

There was this sort of weather setting in for a time. Dusk made the gaping buildings doleful. Sarah took her tea inside. By accident she let her face empty. And Theo saw, and mistaking the expression for sadness pushed his hand against hers, over the top of it, to clasp.

75

Oh honey.

Do you get to claim 'tragic' as a core emotion?

What she would have spent her money on.

Wads of money promised out of nothing. Blood money. Money from death.

She counted his bruises and kissed them and that was a lie.

You should have been a good girl, successful, but let's face it.

Mermaids wait pruning preening in the water between murders.

The sky tinges with blood and it's a play and you are luminescent together in grief and gold.

How did the two dollar *Show of Passion* end?

Oh yes—

The director pressing his head into his clammy hands. Sandwiches and liquefied organs. Rewrite the story. Instead let all pathetics be crisp as a new banknote. Why was that so hard? Be unkind to other people's mothers. Be ungracious when no one expects it. Break down and cry with a mouthful of food at a stranger's table, whatever. You take the stage. You instead press against the actor and become surfaces. Two bright luminescent things that no one can touch. And then you burst into brilliant flame, right, and consummate, consume and never never let anyone know the place in your head where the bones don't join.

Sarah let Theo undress her. He peeled off the top layers then faced the bra she had chosen. A pattern of yellow roses. She flipped the back free, but he made no move to take it away. At the side of her vision the lush, glowing colour of the pile of her clothes. She didn't ask him anything. The way in which he tried a little to nudge the bra strap back up her arm was couched in sadness. Jesus, just stop that, she thought.

She looked at him through her eyelashes, she reached for his shirt and felt his warm skin. Her fingers found the top button on his jeans. And then stopped. He also froze, hands halfway to unzipping himself and shifted away to ferret for a condom. Sarah moved up to catch him as he turned and to roll it on him herself.

And they fought to each other's mouths

and she jabbing fingers into his hair,

pushing him inside her, cold and ribbed and then not noticeably so.

And then the usual soft urging cajoling kisses noises touches rocking motions in the hollows. And she fled into her body. Fell and fell into it. But Theo was vague and timid. His hand holding hers back from returning to his hair, his head moving slightly out of contact with her kisses. She pushed his head nearer. She wanted to snarl and grunt but his movements were like fine glass, like a long corridor with the ending obscured.

They fell asleep apart. Sarah half woke to feel his arms were around her, clamping. And she, a closed eye, pulled the sleeping bag over them, to sweat under it, stifled.

76

It was black out and Theo was missing.

Sarah held off calling for him. Until time passed and he did not come back. She felt an empty wetness between her legs. And angry. Both those things in the flesh of her. She fingered for the zipper of the door this time. No guiding hand against hers. She pushed her bare neck and arms and breasts out. Outside no stars, nothing at all.

'Theo?' she whispered.

Nothing.

A branch cracking,

A wave hitting the shore of the dead lake many miles distant.

She licked her teeth and was in the howling desert nothing,

and became without the moon a monster walking across night's sharp grass.

What she would say later

It had been the sound of a large animal attacking a smaller one, and that smaller one screaming, screaming. And then of an echo of running across dry packed earth on legs that disagreed with the body. On three legs, on one. Thrash of bones breaking as into the undergrowth a shrieking thing fell and tumbled against rock. Blooded shocks. No moment to place them nor halt a terrifying speed.

A strange silhouette on the top of the hill, a sound, a series of awful sounds.

Sarah dragged the groaning body. The palm of her hand was all cut up, and she was rigid. Back up the hill. Each step. Down to the car, to get him into the car. The doctors would want to know, the police, local hunters. Attack by bear, or mountain lion, a wolf. A vengeful Cold War Ghost.

Or Sarah herself.

She blinked. She looked at her hands bleeding on the steering wheel.

The man in the back was silent.

A silver car braked ahead, banked left to Española, the centre of the New World. But the map said there were two ways, more or less equidistant. Sarah felt the glow of town ahead on the flats, whooshing nearer. The bright boxes of the fastfood places, the drive thru, the liquor warehouse.

Española Hospital, six miles, affiliated with a particular branch of Christianity. She pleaded with the God of desert monsters that Theo would not be sent away. Theo lay curled in the back seat bleeding. On the icy fringe of waking. He whimpered as the lights of the hospital finally stroked his face.

There would never again be that time before all this had begun.

Just like the last time.

In the waiting room all the details were white and plastic and behind that chaos. Sarah touched her hair. The ends were wet slicked. Her hair had fallen in a sweep against Theo's chest. It was now his hair, stuck together with his fluids.

She sat on a wipe-clean chair and looked down at the stain on her chambray shirt. A sprawl of blood, a glossy transfer. She touched that, and found it wet and tacky also. She hovered a pencil over the form the receptionist had given her and began to scrawl answers and erase them and write them in again. She had no idea what she was writing. She was writing wild vine leaves and a labyrinth of rust-coloured bricks, she wrapped this in a moat of the Rio Grande. She looked at her hands pink with blood padded with dressing and wondered if it was rude of her to sit like this, near intact.

She straightened her back. The world swam white. She had Theo's sad little gold watch. It was perfectly fine and said 4am. No one else was around but people doing their jobs. This was an American hospital and spoke medicine in a different language to the one Sarah knew. For example, in the language of money in exchange for repair. And here she had forms to fill in and everything was blank. Gam knew about all this. She needed to call Gam. She looked down at the clipboard again, where she had pencilled in some degree of identity:

Theodore Coronado sex male.

Was there anything else she knew? That he was charismatic and forceful when it didn't matter and weak when it did. That his hair curled and was charming. That he was a little boy who had lost someone whose watch he still wore. That he'd had no idea of why she had walked so steadily towards him and bent down to pick up a long dagger of glass while he pissed against the wall of the barracks and how she had awaited his turning around and jagged that glass deep into his belly. Looking each other in the eyes. Hand over hand. And all he might not remember. The yowling and the feeble run. His fall amid rocks. Her perfect stillness for a moment and warmth as if this was all she had ever wanted. To ruin, to watch someone else be broken open outside in real time.

She wrote:

Coronado residence, Valles Grande, nr Este, New Mexico.

Gam could do this. Tomorrow, she would call then. Aware she would wash up against tomorrow half dead and sticky and blood-caked and ugly and perhaps a murderer. But anyway. She'd call tomorrow.

She took up the form and waited. At first, there was only the name tag on a pink flowered uniform. Then the receptionist's face pulling into focus. A big, neat woman with large comfortable arms. Reddish-brown hair that lay in pencil rows, brought into a thick ponytail.

'Okay, hun. You know, there's a coffee machine down the hall, and the vending machine has candy, sandwiches, coke, if you need anything.' A deep voice, now used in kindness. It might easily be so stern it could crack apart the earth.

Sarah nodded, walked off. The way the receptionist had said the word sandwiches, Sarah carried the warmth of that against her chest. Hunger was a long way off, but she could still look.

Sarah walked with small steps and hunched. The hallway stirred around her. Familiar industrial smell and bright shabbiness. It would still be dark outside, though there were no windows by which to judge. On the left and on the right all those doorways led to rooms of supplies. Others to rooms of monitoring machinery and support machinery and white beds with the inhabitants painfully, dully awake, or fitfully sleeping, or forever sleeping. Rooms from the army barracks; open wires graffiti emptiness detached.

At the corner of the corridor there were two pots of coffee

on a heated stand. She made it over to the stand, poured half a cup and sipped it black. Black taste like eating dirt. If you are ailing eat coal coke mixed with a little beef tea. That was in a book Lucy had read out to her. Next to the coffee stand was the vending machine, diagonally opposite the vending machine, a stainless steel payphone. And more and more glossy blue doors continuing down the length of the windowless hall. After the point at which it right-angled, presumably more rooms still. The architecture of a hospital performs a simple trap for sickness.

Sarah wondered if anyone would come after her, should she wander away. She would not wander away. She did not wonder the why of anything. She took her coffee back to the white room to sit awhile continuing to balance on nothing.

79

The grounds of a hospital. It was '98 or '99. Spring, and the lawn had been so lush that handfuls of blackbirds and bluetits bounced off it when they tried to land and whipped back into the branches of lime trees in bud. Daisies embroidered the fringes. Sarah was coming to see Aunt Selene, who lay in a great big bed with brass fittings. This was a bed for well people, and there was Aunt Selene looking up from it, with no tubes or machinery beside her, only a small red alarm clock, the kind that doesn't tick when people are speaking and ticks like death when the room is empty. A clock to make Selene get up in good time for her treatments.

Cousin Lucy had flicked at the clock. That fact, for some reason, Sarah always remembered. Lucy was now thirty-one and had never destroyed anyone and had been successful in London and life in all the ways Sarah had failed. But that day teenage Lucy had put on one of Selene's overlong little black dresses and a smidge too much makeup so that her face took up too much room. And then the face was spidery black and smeary from her rare, awkward crying.

'I don't want to see her, I won't see her,' Lucy had protested halfway from Falmouth to that meadowy brooked Edwardian estate. Maud at the wheel had simply told her in rigorous detail what exactly was wrong with Aunt Selene, how much she had drank for how many days, how a strange man had found her in his house, and no one could explain how she'd got in there. How terribly swollen up her liver was and how decayed and dehydrated that brain in that little round skull of hers. Like a ball of pinky grey rubber bands, creaky and this close to tearing themselves apart.

Sarah hated all of them. She had sat neatly in the car and neatly by Selene's bedside. She had kept a fine hate, like magma under the earth. Of course her hatred was of no interest to anyone else, but she was young and hate was her only weapon. Her rage sheathed up to its hilt in her chest so the blade would never rust. Hate with no object now. Hate that finds out the object.

But in '98 or '99, Lucy all blotchy and yellow haired had stood over her mother asking that she try to get better soon. Selene had smiled in her usual way, saying, 'As long as my dear family keep reaching out to me, I shall always be on the mend, shan't I?' Lucy had brushed her mother's hair. She'd helped her put on a dressing gown and smiling, walked her to the window, bearing all her mother's faint, needling remarks. Sarah seethed. Took all the anger that should have been in her cousin and bore that. She came to think of herself as a catchment, an essential part. But that was not true. She was like the clothes that sat now so easily over her body. Like the figure that her mother painted. Like the sheets that covered Aunt Selene. Something that ought to be cast off, bleached, and hung out on a glorious morning that burned after the fog.

The three wellish people had gone out to wander among the beeches, sharing a bag of bacon-flavoured crisps.

'Revolting,' Maud had said, 'but so moreish. Hmm, Lucy, Sarah. Don't dawdle quite so much. You know, until the doctor gives Selene her gold star, it's just us, and we shall be reckless. Crisps, and beef every night. Black market beef-on-the-bone. I know someone who can get us any cut we like. Our brains will be utterly scrambled by CJD rot by the end of the month.'

Maud Browne, little, and wicked. In a heavy forest green coat over a bright green cardigan fastened to the throat, and on the coat collar a pearl brooch, which you remember well. She wore that brooch at the last Midnight Mass you went to together. White pearl green cardigan small strides picking up her feet as if the ground was not worthy of her fierce, fastidious step. Descriptors Sarah threw at that woman like glass throws itself from windows. Mum. Mum, who was dead. Everyone dies. Everyone passes out of reach. It is very simple, until it happens. Now that you set it down you realise.

80

Sarah sat with her coffee in her hands. Smoothly the hospital moved around her. Later in '99, rain was falling against the library windows. The ceiling never dripped in the library. Lucy and Sarah were practicing black magic. They sat within a circle of candles reading Tarot cards to find out nothing in particular. About boys, perhaps. The question of death is too great to be asked, and so it doesn't get asked. Also it is a bit boring. With eyes closed Sarah laid out the cards in one of the prescribed spreads. The Tarot reader had been a Christmas present for Lucy. Sarah was enthralled by the image on the cover of a woman holding out her arms. Her bland but yearning expression and disarrayed folds of her dress with one breast exposed. Sarah around that time had started laying things out within herself, turning over each thought, trying to work out what it signified. All she knew then was that everyone around her was either dying all the time or Lucy. She wanted to be like the woman on the cover. All heavy and languid and leaning against a milky pillar with no one at all to wind her up.

'You look like a horse, doing that with your lips,' Lucy said, laughing, throwing a pillow at her, scattering the cards.

We talk of the rain lashing the windows but it only happens in the past. Years and years ago the rain lashed the windows and the roses outside were shaken so hard that in the morning they had all lost their heads. And the petals were mauve and primrose yellow and lilac, because colours are important.

Forgive them, Sarah. Or do not forgive. Does forgiveness require from its deliverer that they must be inherently forgivable too? Sarah sat bloody in a hospital in New Mexico in the flood of her lostness. She answered her cousin, peering at her over candle light.

'Yes I do look like a horse, quite right,' she said, 'and if I am a horse, you have to be one too. You just show differently. Yours is a horse bum. Better stop eating or we'll have to make you into glue.'

It was years later, it was thousands of unforgiving miles distant, and it was fucking ridiculous to be sad, covered in blood, to mourn the little that was: childhood, the Warne, with Lucy.

In the past you had so much potential for something. You were always building up to it. Can you forgive potential? Name it from a textbook and forgive it that way. Or white out the consequences before they happen. A girl like a war is always ongoing. Often denied to be so. If someone bothered to press their ear to the skin they would have heard it there a constant droning sound.

81

Sarah put away her coffee cup; she had bitten pieces out of the lip of it and let them fall white in the dregs.

'Would Ms Browne please come to the reception in the ER, would Ms Browne please—'

At the reception desk, the woman behind the counter was consulting some papers and speaking to another woman – tall and white-coated, obviously very tired.

'I'm Sarah Browne. Is this about Theodore Coronado?'

'Yeah, of course,' said the doctor. 'We need to see if there are any next of kin available. We just tested, and he has a rare blood type. It makes transfusions harder. It would help if someone from his family could travel here within the next hour or so –' the doctor broke off in a yawn, 'sorry, anyway, going to need any contact numbers, if you have them.'

She would check the car, she said, forgetting she had Gam's number on her phone. Outside the air was sharp though the sun was beginning to come up beyond the car park. It broke in pretty beams through some trees above a thread of the Grande.

Sarah's eyes watered. Her hand ached and probably needed tending with painkillers. Her eyes wobbled when she touched the gash. But she would not ask. She peeled back the dressing and stared at the red, thinking she should probably reopen and harm the wound every time it healed. Or salt the edges. Salt like glass flakes, salt shards from the actual sea.

In the car Sarah found Theo's wallet, just as she remembered her phone. She flipped the wallet open anyway and took out the contents. Cards, receipts. Something to shuffle as she waited. She walked through the hospital doors and handed the receptionist Gam's number written down on a coffee discount card. She sat back down on the plastic chair. What do the cards say of the man they belong to? Visa. A loyalty card for a bookshop in Albuquerque. That he liked coffee and liked reading. The cards are reticent. They do not reveal their secrets to those who will not look with due scrutiny. An organ donation card. Here is the Hanged Man. Here is Death, who marks a change from one state to another. From wholeness to piercedness. A folded but newish photograph of a beautiful bearded man. The Hermit. Who signifies – who signifies – but she had forgotten. One of those flat rectangular penknives designed to fit in a wallet.

Sarah slid out the fittings of the knife; paring blade, scissors, set of compasses as thin as a dove's wishbone. The pen was missing and there was an empty slot for what might have been tweezers. You cannot write your body down, you cannot pluck it out. Pluck it out from what? Remove it to where? NM driver's licence. Supermarket receipt. An out-of-date hunting licence. He is prepared to kill what he loves. A little shudder of respect and gun loathing. Staff library card for Albuquerque. The cards spoke, they told her he would not easily forget. But really, there was no way to know the right interpretation. There always is an interpretation. You can choose to lie or you can choose the truth, but you are free to do either, no matter what anyone says. No one is watching that closely.

The doctor returned with Sarah's phone.

'We couldn't get through to Theodore's mom. But we'll keep trying.'

'Yes,' Sarah said. 'Georgiana Coronado,' Sarah said.

'Not Gam, okay.' The doctor said, and turned to leave. Yes Gam, but also Georgiana. To you.

'And how is he?'

'Well, stable,' said the doctor. 'He'll improve a lot once we do a transfusion. There may be a risk of secondary infections. But it looks like he fell on a glass shard, so that's unlikely. Metal would have been a problem.'

'Do you know how it happened?'

'I'm hoping we can get Theodore to tell us himself.' The doctor smiled in an encouraging way. 'I can't tell you too much more, but I can tell you, you did good, bringing him in all by yourself. It must have been difficult.'

'No, not that difficult. I really felt responsible,' said Sarah.

The doctor smiled again. 'Well. If you need a cup of coffee, there's a stand down the hall.'

82

The waitress set down a beige plate of pancakes with slices of banana and fake cream and said coffee would be there in just a tick. Food has its own small grace. She'd taken money for this grace from Theo's wallet because he had said he would help with the petrol. Theo was in a white bed somewhere. Sarah hadn't waited around to speak to Gam because the doctor was going to do it. You're doing well. You don't feel too much of anything. Balance.

There was a tin jug of syrup beside the plate and she tried to pour some out. But the syrup gave off a strong slick copper smell and it fell with hypnotic slowness. The syrup wasn't syrup, it was a red and viscous hybrid of blood and syrup. The tip of the syrup-blood tongue oozed over the top pancake. Sarah watched it calmly until it was just syrup again, and too much of it. It left a grim trail on the body of the jug. Sarah moved the jug far away and began to eat.

The waitress placed a coffee cup down. This strong careful action was a form of continuity, a link to everyone in the diner. The waitress had earlier placed the mug down in front of an old man with a milky eye and a crumpled fedora. And another mug in front of a large lady in a dolphin tee-shirt. Slopped it a little in front of the most beautiful man the waitress had ever seen. Lowered it with more delicacy before a woman with three sand-haired kids hitting one another with plastic dinosaurs. Waitresses were holier than doctors, or at least their rituals were simpler. Simpler, and performed with wholesome things and not with opened bodies.

Sarah had changed into a man's plaid shirt, at the waitress's insistence. There was a box of these things, though the waitress had not explained why. Sarah assumed it was because bloodied visitors from the hospital were a regular enough occurrence that something ought to be done, for goodness sake. She had asked for and been given a plastic bag for the preservation of her bloodied articles.

Sarah tilted cream into the cup, thinking she would never love what the thickness of cream did to the texture. And also that she would be sure to tip generously with Theo's money. She watched how the morning occupied the room. And how through an opening in the wall she could see the fry cooks moving about ministering to the breakfasts of people they'd never see. Pan clatter, leap of oiled flames. A woman rasped loudly into her phone at the far end of the restaurant, 'Where the hell is my car? Jesus, they're still looking at it? Anyways. There's no change in Frank. You gonna bring me my list? Yeah. I'm going nowhere.'

Sarah cut up her pancakes into irregular triangles then ate the banana slices off the top of them first. Her mouth filled with a sense of community, a sense that if she chose to speak to anyone here they would understand that smooth tide that had briefly engulfed her and now receded and that everything was fine.

Theo lay connected to the world by flimsy lines, an astronaut suspended above the curvature of the Earth. Sarah presumed it must be dark in his head, like space, and wondered if in all that immensity he was afraid. If he were capable of fear in his current state. She moved her finger so that it was lightly touching his fingernail. That seemed ridiculous. To say she was sorry in that way. But she knew no other way that worked, and most people are too conscious to let you close enough to ask by touch. And, too, she was asking herself something. It was midday and the blinds were patting rhythmically against the window.

The moment you realise you are in love will have a sound to it like the music of the spheres. That is, totally silent, or above human hearing, and immense, and real, and you are suddenly aware of how little air has been going in and out of your chest for so many months or years or forever, how now the air is filling you up with uncountable galaxies and unfathomable force, and you will break apart from it. But here there was nothing. The blinds, the studious machinery. Sarah removed her finger from his.

She stood over Theo awhile. At least there was gentleness now, at least there was proximity. It didn't kill you, she thought. It wasn't meant to.

The Warne in a young summer. Up the wooden staff staircase from the kitchen, tapping the photograph of the maids for luck – big eyed girls in white caps and black dresses, Warne behind them, all very keen, all very dead. On the second landing a narrow twist leads to a broad, decorous corridor of dark wood and pale green walls. The rooms along it have been always locked. So you go as fast as you can, slapping your naked feet on the boards to the good bathroom, the one without collapsing pipes and with fewer spiders.

Open the big black door. There Sarah is sitting in the claw-footed tub, submerged in bubbles and glitter. There too is Lucy in a neat blue seventies tunic, perched on the toilet seat, trying to find a poem from the anthology in her lap.

You can't just bathe every time you feel like it. It costs far too much to fill, and in any case the ceramic is horribly cracked and sometimes catches the skin. It's Sarah's twelfth birthday. That afternoon comes in through the open bathroom window, blowsy with the scent of a hundred flowers and salt. Pink bubblegum water under the bubbles. Sarah holds a bowl of home-picked cherries dangerously close to the water's edge. She puts three in her mouth at once and begins the complicated act of chewing around the pits.

Lucy begins:

'Dark house, by which once more I stand
Here in the long unlovely street,
Doors, where my heart was used to beat
So quickly, waiting for a hand,

A hand that can be clasped no more –
Behold me, for I cannot sleep,
And like a guilty thing I creep
At earliest morning to the door…'

Sarah finishes her mouthful and scowls. 'That's not a love poem. Well done, congratulations. You found the worst love poem in the history of all time.'

'It's by Alfred, Lord Tennyson and you don't know what you're talking about. You're twelve, birthday girl, and you're sulking in the bath.'

'It's about someone who died. It's not a love poem when the person is dead. I'm supposed to be having a treat for my birthday and you're reading to me about dead people and being in the street too early. You're rubbish.'

All of a sudden the door clatters and in strides Maud. Brown hair full of gold, a puff of red from the sun on her cheek. She peers at her daughter as if struggling to remember who this creature is and if she was formally invited or had sneaked in to use the facilities. It is summertime and she has been drinking with her sister out on the lawn since lunch. Pimm's, white wine, art talk. No kiddies allowed. After her moment of surprise, she puts her hands on her hips.

'Gosh, it looks like you're bleeding and clouding up the water with it. How grim.'

'It's a bubble bath. There's glitter and I think it looks nice.'

'Oh absolutely, absolutely. One day, I'll show you that painting of the suicide in the bath, awful, very baroque – I can't recall the name right now.' And then she pauses, turns on her heels, wanders out leaving the door ajar. Her small back receding, the unhurried tick of her heels, the slight stagger as she bumps against the wall at the turn.

To be fair she had wished Sarah a very happy birthday darling at the breakfast table, and given her a new sketchpad from the studio.

But Lucy's present had been good. It had been. Words and

a pretty pink bubble bath. But because of Maud's lax, callous way, now there are all those neurons stained pink stained death in Sarah's sweet pre-anger pre-adolescent head.

It was a long time after, in New Mexico.

Sarah, hair plaited, sat in carnation print flannel pyjamas. She was drinking tea in her kitchen as snow padded the outer sill and glass of the windows. The light was diffuse. It was a beautiful moment of repose. Weeks and weeks ago she had almost killed Theo and now the air out on the back porch stung her nostrils.

She faced the whiteout and was deciding whether it was worth getting dressed in order that she might have more powdered milk and a treat of clementines from the supermarket.

Scratch the paint from this life and there is another beneath: in which Sarah was striding across the Valle towards Theo's house. It took no effort in thought. She knocked on the door, and then there was the briefest pause. Theo hobbling downstairs to answer and open the screen door, parting his lips in sorrow and welcome.

His voice would be quiet, hoarse. She had not heard him speak since the last day at the hospital. He would have let his stubble grow into a dark beard. Now he must look haunted and stern. The kind of beauty that is found in heroes of novels set in wartime, in countries that have long since been broken up like biscuits. Would he still lean on the doorframe, would he still give off an air of impenetrability? There are photos of men taken before and after life has done a cruel thing to them. The immortal prettiness of a young man nervous before the camera, then that same face as soldier. That same face after the sight of death has removed something from them. What is it? Sarah thought that is the kind of art that matters, a journalistic art she had never been taught. It might be she had never seen the before picture of Theo, not really. She was thinking of the unfamiliar picture in his wallet.

Anyway, she would tell him, right there on the doorstep that she had come to realise her awfulness. And would not ask to be forgiven because forgiveness is a violent act of mercy against the past. It was a request asked of another's soul, and she had no right and as a monster maybe had no soul herself. If evil is a human thing, blank cruelty is the monster's remit. After that delivery, she would do nothing else but walk away across the crisp and gleaming snow in a scene that we always read despite ourselves as representing absolution.

She touched the scar in her right hand. If it was possible to be guilty and at peace, then she was. All her anger had gone into that night. That meant she felt little, day to day. She was not hollow, but was definitely not entirely herself. Like a pine struck by lightning. Smooth and upright and somewhat natural despite the ravage but a dead thing nevertheless.

She had gone to pick Theo up on the day of his discharge. Gam's car 'in the shop, of all the times for the carburettor to go'. She had found him in the waiting area on the same seat where she had been, looking away and all bandaged up. Crooked in his mannerisms. Now friendly enough, an arm against an arm. Now coldness towards her. Did he remember or did he not.

They had gone to the car.

'I bled for days,' he had said.

His tee-shirt with the blood transfer had been thrown out. She had to keep her chambray shirt wrapped in a plastic bag. The smell of it heady. Like syrup, like mornings where you wake up having ruined the world, a little glass in your pocket, knackered fists. Bloodied articles about your person like a confession you reveal over and over to yourself. Is this how Protestant Christians might do it? A Confrontational.

It was not true, what Theo had said. So she had smiled, and returned with 'No. It must have seemed a long time, from when you fell to when they got to work on you. But I think you were not terribly aware for most of it.'

'I don't remember, I remember waking up a lot and you weren't there.'

'I was there,' Sarah had said, slotting the key in the ignition, 'I took you to the hospital, and I stayed with you, sometimes left Gam alone with you.'

In her cabin in her pyjamas, Sarah could remember what she had been wearing, which was a green something and a grey something, but not what had happened, not the texture of anything she had touched that day. But one thing – the way Theodore Coronado had smelled like a person does when they come out of a hospital. A little like antibiotic hand wash, but mostly like nothing of himself, like a replicant.

Sarah listened to her fingers tapping on the keyboard, their echo against the wooden walls. The money had come through into her English bank account, minus the required taxes and other fees. She had entered into a correspondence with a small art gallery in Shoreditch and the reply was giving her trouble.

After Theo's release she had gone into the woods and tried to replicate the chambray shirt and what it meant. She had taken a stack of ugly plates up to the woods where she had broken them into pieces, seeking in the cracks and the cuts she gave herself and bloody fingers and bursts of tiny sickening yelps, a leavening. She took pictures of the strewn stuff as it was amongst the unthreaded needles of pine and many little sticks. And thinking, this makes it better, this sort of transfer and not the other, though she couldn't be sure.

These photos and the ones of the raptured clothing had twinged the dick of the Shoreditch gallery owner. A friend a few times removed. Like all Sarah's friends. Thank you for your interest in my empty clothes. Artist statement. I think the prints will sell well. I think people will easily remember them. I think this small amount of text on the wall beside them will make them meaningful. She sent the email and stared at her fire, humming a song in a bubblegum key. After some time, her pink fingers brushed about below the waistband of her pyjamas, then caressed, because she was warm there, harsh furred and wet. Who did she think of? The snow outside, falling. Half a song lyric, over and over. The image of delicate eyes and chest fuzz. She came in a quiet and nearly painful way. When she pulled out her hand there was blood on it. You're fine Sarah. You are right here. Your body is fine.

She leaned forward to sip some tea. She might get dressed and leave for town in an hour or so.

86

'How did it happen?'

It had been the third night, or it was the fourth, at the hospital. The room with the blind shades, one bed, two cushioned yellow-brown chairs. Gam leaned forward, hawkish.

'You said you went out there to see ruined stuff.'

'Yes, I said that.'

'And this was right after you snuck up and killed my plants.'

'Yes.'

'Go get me a coffee. And a cheese sandwich. I want to stay here with him. Don't be quick.'

That conversation like something out of a bedtime story, blunt, but rife and gleaming.

'Do you think he'll be better soon?' Sarah had asked upon returning.

'No,' answered Gam. 'No. And he'll be like my others, if he doesn't pull through.'

Sarah had looked at a linoleum corner of the room. The corner had a neatness where it met the wall. It was trying to be reassuring.

'I had four,' Gam had said, 'I guess, not technically four. Two wouldn't count to a girl like you.'

Sarah thinking about this thought to say, well, my mother died not long ago, do you hear me bragging? Do you think Theo will be there, hand on yours, when you're dying? And did Gam even think at all or just make pronouncements.

Sarah's eyes had hurt from being open too long. You forget to blink in hospitals. She didn't know if she had spoken or not. The room was too pale and dim and it would be nice to be clean and in her own clothes again. Orange night outside. Concrete. Was the diner open? Sarah had gathered herself, clutching green bills. Stood. On the way out, she turned.

'Do they make you pay the hospital bill, if he dies?' She had almost felt obliged to say it.

After a time, Gam responded, 'You're like a stone, you have this stoniness to you, you know that?'

Sarah had held silent.

'Well, you're not, missy. You are not a stone. You got no defence.'

Sarah distinctly remembered lifting first one foot, placing it a little further back, then the other foot, a little further back. That slight squeak of the linoleum is the most affecting noise of a hospital. More than the machines making their dutiful sounds. More than the murmurs of cars outside, escaping.

87

'What have you been doing this last week then? How's school?'
Maud lay on her side, holding Sarah's hand. They were in
cahoots behind heavy plastic curtains. The rest of the ward
room was asleep, enjoying a painless moment on a warm
afternoon.

'Nothing much. School's always the same. I did all right in
my essay about Larkin though.'

'I thought you would. Did you go with my suggestion?'

'Went with "Aubade". Teacher thinks I'm a bit grim now.
Anyway. Lucy's been trying the new Delia. She made some
gingerbread.'

'Oh, and was it good?'

'No, it was horrible. She forgot the ginger! And it was too
dry. We tried to feed it to the birds and they wouldn't eat it.'

Maud did her sick-person laugh, a silent shake of mirth.

'Is it better if I move this?' said Sarah, holding one corner of
the pillow, 'or…'

'Don't fuss, Sarah. Yes, a bit.'

It was always, 'yes fine,' or 'no, leave it where it is,' 'stop
fussing.' The room with the blinds ticking against the window,
the counterpane, a red patchwork quilt Maud brought in to the
hospital with her.

The edges melt away. The heart fussing. The hairbrush with
the last pale hairs. Brickwork on the wall, covered in lichens.
From the walled garden a smell of apple blossom.

'I'm not stony, am I, Mum? Gam thinks I'm like a stone.'

'Well, a little, now. But you weren't always. That woman
doesn't know you at all.' Maud squeezed her hand. There was a
blood stain on the quilt between them, cherry red. 'I'm awfully
tired now. I'm tired of being your prop. I'm tired of how much
blood there always is.'

On the day she had injured her mother Sarah had stayed behind in the Warne while the rest had hurried out to the A&E. It had been the last ever time she had felt happy there. Wandering about with a mug of tea in her uninjured hand. The silence of fledness following her through each corridor. Into the pantry where they kept biscuit tins from the 1920s. Full of dried herbs from the garden. It all smelled so good, the empty house. The phone had rung and rung. But in the pantry, leaning her back on the shelves, Sarah had closed her eyes. Grand, safe, awful.

She told her mother about it, in the hospital in her head. Not asking for the guilt to be mopped up. Just telling her.

'I don't know now how to have done the right thing back then. I always tell myself there's too much violence in me. Where or what violence is I don't know. Is it a force or is it an emotion or a movement of the muscles or what. While you're here, can I ask about forgiveness? What that is too, or how to go about it, from either approach.'

'It doesn't matter, does it? You just were saying it was nearly impossible. Now you're asking me. I mean, I'm dead. That's the end to that. What could I possibly tell you?'

'Should I talk it out with Theo? I wonder if he knows. He didn't say a thing. He seems changed, but he would. After the incident, after me. I think Gam would come over and beat me to death with her knotty little fists if she knew—'

Maud closed her eyes.

They were walking over the heath where the barrow stood.

Now in the Warne's sunken ballroom where the spiders came peeping out of the shiny, rotten floor.

Now with the dressing-up box. We are putting on a play, this is the play, please write the review and post it in the kitchen and we will make improvements for the next show. Love, Sarah and Lucy.

Now the back door opens with such ferocity. It can be no one else.

'Fucking rain,' Maud says with cheer, throttling her

umbrella. Two months no Mum, now Mum is here. Sarah standing at the door in her pyjamas, shy and very happy, then running forward for a hug.

'Not now, Sarah, for goodness sake, I'm soaking. And I just got back from the most wearying trip.'

Now it is London on a sleety November morning. You are walking by the river pretending all the luxurious buildings are just for you and feeling like you might be accepted anywhere.

'No, I didn't invite you,' Maud's hesitant broken voice, 'I don't tell people I have a daughter, only if they ask. It leads to awkwardness. I don't think I'd like you to come, Christmas or not.'

The black shell of the phone in her hand. 2002, back when it might have been fixed.

Now April of 2005. Temp job. Long a drop-out from the art school and crumpled over a keyboard, whispering. Begging. And three years after that, Maud in the hospital, croaking into the phone as Lucy held it.

'Well, we've agreed that's just how it has to be. Given everything. I just can't. I love you and I can't.'

And now all that money, all that signed over to her as if in severance pay.

You might still have a self to find, have a life to recover. A human being made up of shards and broken lines. It's quite funny really. If someone asked her to relate her life to them, she'd have to laugh. She'd put her arms around them and just laugh low. Oh, I've had to be grand, hon. I've had to be fucking awful.

Now you just see a slip of a woman, small frame pale brown hair, sidling through traffic. Watch out, lady. She doesn't look back, doesn't slow, but that's entirely to be expected. One day you might catch up.

88

It was ten minutes later, perhaps, Sarah had lost track of time.

She pulled on leggings and a long green skirt, an arrangement of three cardigan layers. Her hair was getting too long and hissed from dryness at the ends. She walked around her house, picking at the edges of the bookcase, the undersides of the counters. Something in her chest had risen, blocking the air. It was the cabin itself; she had swallowed it. She stood in the cabin inside her throat, at the kitchen window, she crouched and shunted bottles under the sink. She walked through rooms, looking for objects that seemed to confirm some horror of weight. A tonne of splintering pine and tile, inside and surrounding her. A pair of marigold gloves, musty and bloated. She clutched them, bent down and threw them on the fire in the stove. A previously unnoticed whorl in the wood looked at her with an open-mouthed expression. A gouged, mask-like face with two pitiless eyes. She lay down on the living room floor, first staring at the whorl, then turned away. The fire roasted her back. If for an unbearable period, everything is spite. What then? Then latex, stinking.

Then, slowly, a sort of dispersal.

She was up. Opened a window and went upstairs. She sat calmly in front of an internet tutorial on how to make a chignon and managed an acceptable version, tucking the edges of her hair under. She made a sloppy red bow of her lips. In the interim between sliding towards panic and rising to the laptop she had chosen the way to defend herself against an increasingly hostile existence, which was to go to Paris for Christmas, alone. And she had not bought a return ticket. Her hotel was in Bastille, on a street with a man's name. The eleventh Arrondissement. Why there particularly, out of all of Paris. Out of all the world? Shh.

One morning Sarah had packed away her things without ceremony and saw to the latching of doors, the turning off of switches. She put on her winter things, she told no one where she was going. Because, once again, there was no one really to tell.

In Denver airport and then JFK she had checked in and waited the hours, reading a magazine and a second, drinking coffee until her stomach hurt. She had slept the night in the air. Everything held. Everything passed by. The window seat looked out on the milk stew of clouds, the high altitude sun shone on the pale wing of the plane and on her skin alike. Her luggage had gone around on the carousel, pathetically crooked, one wheel spinning. And at last she had sat in a taxi as it raced through Paris, and peered at the irongrey citiness, quiet. She had let herself fall in and out of a sequence of dazes. Thoughts of winter, white cloud, the money that she would now let shield her.

Sarah's room. It was not the kind of hotel room one sees in films of Paris. It was tastefully demure in slate greys with accents of lily-orange in the soft furnishings. She moved to pick up her coat from the back of a chair, but hesitated. The excess of vibrant pillows had begun to grate. Sarah walked around the room taking them up. And looked to the window. She felt the strongest desire to throw the pillows out the window. To simultaneously rid herself of them and let a scatter of raw silk offset the tensed quality of the street below. It would be easy. Everything dreamlike and easy. She settled for tossing out a single face towel, made also of silk, for fuck's sake, and watched it flutter gaudily down onto the roof of a silver car.

89

Sarah looked up at the golden angel. She held a crêpe that warmed her hands, taking very small bites and carefully licking the hazelnut chocolate off her fingers. Every route seemed to take her back here, to Place de la Bastille. To the golden angel at the top of the Colonne de Juillet. She took her continual return as an act of approval. For her boldness. For the shedding of the past. There are so many acts can seem revolutionary these days.

She moved on, stopping to take a photograph on her phone of a man juggling with a goldfish in a bowl balanced on his head. And in pausing realised that she had been a little sarcastic with herself. Settling her feelings should be simple. Especially when she had singled everything down to this. Everything ought to be translucent. Aren't you happy, Sarah? It is a radical act of self-love to tell yourself you are happy. Look where you are.

She clicked down the steps of the Métro. She had decided to go shopping, because being rich was a process of uncovering what it meant to be rich; what trappings suited her. No, that was not right. What aspect she wished to present. And it was Christmas, the best time to shop for yourself. All those around you are on the sour brink, frantically shuffling through the shelves for something, anything, that will not make them look like lousy fuckwits to their beloved. But your warm scarf is at your throat, the salesgirl helps you browse, pitying you just the right amount and flattering you to smooth the way.

On the Champs-Élysées she went from store to store. Beiges and deep carpet and glass. Leather bags embossed with the snick of privilege. But after a time it grew harder. Twice she tried to walk in and instead retreated. An invisible barrier had formed. You can always make yourself want the goods. She looked in through the window at scarves with little horses in yellow all over them like a rash. They cost more than she had earned in a day making coffee. And it would be easy enough to toss her card at the sales assistant, dash out again bescarved.

All down the length of the Champs-Élysées she felt it. She walked on by that display and the next, limp, hesitant. How about breaking the window, taking the log display, putting on the necklace, the many bracelets and the watch, and leaving ten grand for the damage? Not a single part of this was real. She might just as well cart the log down the street, crooning to herself, yanks and tangles of gold and silver and her disarranged hair.

She paused at a rubbish bin, looked at the paper bags in her fist. Into the bin they went, crammed through the slot. She stared at the dainty paper handles poking out, one corner of a neon blue purse. A fucking din of thingness. Stay in there, stay far away from me. Two couples passed her by, looking back at her as they did so, though her movements had been slight. Her face fixed and hot. Like dogs can smell fear, the strangers could spot – well, what was it? What feeling was this? Maybe anger. Anger like sugar rush. She coughed and started walking towards the Eiffel Tower, towards the idea of it, waiting for the surge to pass.

Ten minutes later. Down by the Seine. Sarah watched the water, thinking of London. Was she getting any better at any of this? At least today, the idea of throwing herself in and drowning didn't tug at her. Might be an idea to examine why not, and save that reason for a similar day. So she walked down by the river, close to the wall. The water was a pale brown-grey and promised nothing. Quietly slapping the stone bank. There were no observers.

She breathed out white, she felt the gnawing damp, like London, and nostalgia coming on, like pack-ice closing overhead. She felt heavy, with unspoken obligation. Gravity, that was it. Her body saying no. The weight of the world kept her stuck to its surface. Where she crawled. That wasn't a lot to go on, but it seemed to do for the moment.

It was getting late. It was the fourth day or the fifth. The sun's disk was submerging and only her hotel room was waiting for her. A sort of bunker in which she could shut off all the lights and lie down in relative safety, until the next day broke against her with all its dirt and debris.

Sarah wore a new Mackintosh coat, her hair under a warm hat. Lips in a strange nude shade that had made them disappear. Mouthless face. It began to rain as she got out of the Métro at a stop she wanted to think of as Embankment. She was trembling as she crossed the river. Feeling indefinite, at the mercy of. Of every whim. Of the weather, currently.

She walked directly to the green-faced bookshop. Wooden beams, packed shelves and more shelves of books, a tilted chandelier. Shakespeare and Company. Warm, close, looming. She took off her mac and hid her hands in the folds.

It was a mark of how wretched she was that seeing a cat curled up asleep in a box in the corner could make her want to snivel. Ugly, soppy tears. Fuck, she'd let a softness really get into her. More sandbag than girl. To be comforted to the point of breakdown by an old overstuffed bookshop. By the idea that she was buying yet another Christmas present for herself. Like she had done every year for fucking her entire adult life.

Sarah picked up a thin novel from a table beside the counter. *Bonjour Tristesse*. Is that, 'hello sorrow', or is it the city? The book was a dubious choice. Still, she looked around for a place to hunker and get a read of it. There were only the stacks, face out. At this odd morning hour there were maybe two, three other patrons. If any of the employees stopped and tried to talk to her, she could always smile horribly at them with her mouthlessness and buy it anyway, it wouldn't take that much effort.

She paused to rub at her face with a tissue. Not crying but a little damp. She put the tissue away in her handbag and began reading.

'Sin is the only note of vivid colour that persists in the modern world.' She read it and read it again. At first thinking that was the fucking truth. The greys of Paris, beige New Mexico, with its little green sticks of scented trees and bush, mud houses on the flatlands. And then the line unfolded and she began to doubt. The only note of vivid colour. What vivid colour could sin be? The colour of our insides, a yellow sheen. Or the colour of harm. Dark red regret. Sarah closed the book and pushed it into the nearest space on a shelf. The spine of it stared out coolly at her.

Prude.

I'm just trying not to think, she thought.

Of what?

I have to push it away.

Oh yeah, hon? Seems like something you'd do.

Sarah tasted metal at the back of her throat. She put her hand up to her hair. If only she could stop this. Analogies sprouting out of everything. And all she could do was gape at these eruptions of oddness and emotion no one else has the time to even see.

Sarah pulled out *Bonjour Tristesse* and carried it lightly back to the table where it belonged. So, then. Settle yourself. It's just one more outbreak after all. Go and buy a croissant and peel it into tongues for the pigeons. Go and buy a box of Ladurée macarons just to have their pretty box. Stuff yourself with ephemerality. In an alien street, in the frigid rain. Not one gaudy crumb to be left over. Go and buy a cocktail in a black lacquered bar where the liquor is so elegant it chokes you and you like it.

I love Paris, she thought. What tourist doesn't love Paris?

Behind her, the sales assistant had started talking with a couple. All three had American accents. Sarah tuned in. New Yorkers, she thought. She didn't want to hear what they said, just the screwed shape their words made. Wouldn't it be nice if she could solve their query. She could hand them *Bonjour Tristesse*. But they were after something specific, she was sure of it. New Yorkers were a specific people.

She turned her head to eye them. The first man was long

and stoat-like, in a yellow cashmere jumper that didn't look to be to his taste. A gift from the second man? He was a little older, heading into middle age. Thicker in the face, smiled a lot, nodding with curiosity. Not an art crowd, maybe something in publishing, she wasn't sure. The sales assistant had her back to Sarah, but gave a few things away even so. A girl in a dress the colour of a blackboard, very upright, and gesturing with piano player's hands.

You watch and why do you watch? The actions of others are gifts they give, unthinkingly generous. In ways you cannot be. You, watcher. You, violent, guarded, flighty. Sickening on strains of memory. You get so weary. You want to know how not to be, but no one taught you how. Sarah thought, look at these people. They love, they stand together, they shift on their small feet. Why don't I just take their lead. Take a breath, and try for something less shit. Someone laughed, a book changed hands. A set of four white paws walked by, one crooked tail, a flank, a wise wide-eyed face. The cat gently yowled at Sarah. Who was crying now, who was stooping to pet the creature, to hide her face in its short fur.

Paris in austere morning light. Only a visitor can see the whole of a city, make it whole. It is their function. The rumble of a street cleaner. The creak of leather in the interior of a taxi. Wet vinyl flooring smell. The city shrinks as you leave it, but it will regrow, don't worry. Don't even think of it. Feel the churning of your empty stomach. The nearing of return, whatever that is.

The taxi was taking her back to Charles De Gaulle Airport. And from there, JFK, and from there, Denver. Two famous men, one mountain city. She would return to a cabin where she had something to stitch together rightly. To make work. She told herself these points of procedure not for obsession but to confirm in fact this was, would be, her first good choice in many years.

'I won't remember, I'll write it down.'

Sarah woke herself speaking. It was a frigid early afternoon. She listened to her sleeping house. Behind the sofa a window was open letting in a draught that had left motes of snow too broken for snowflakes on her blanket. She might have frozen to death in her sleep. But the world had let her be. She pressed her cold-chapped lips and adjusted her blankets, wanting coffee for herself.

There was a letter waiting by the door. Pure white envelope, apple-white paper.

Sarah,

Got your text. So this is yes. Meet me in the next town over, Dulce's the name of it.
There's a diner on the corner opposite the gate to the hot springs. I'll be there all day thinking and I got a book. Take your time but come soon.

Theo

Snow made a sound like biting into a sugared crust of meringue as she walked over it. Dulce. Sweetness.

Sarah shuddered a sigh, she composed her features. Driving past the sign for the hot springs. And there was the destination; a square block, with fake-adobe frontage and a blue sign lit against the grey light. In the doorway of the diner she shook out her hair. Theo was by the window three booths back and on his face was the wistful, low-eyed stillness most people have while waiting for someone they don't think will show.

Theo looked up briefly. Dark beard, and his curly hair skirting his ears. He held a hardback book propped against the table, which he slid away to one side. A light in the corner of the room had a twitch. Sarah navigated past a table covered in the remains of meals, napkins, and egg-slicked cutlery. An aura of food grease hung in the air and pop country music dirged from the kitchen. She sat down without comment.

'Hey,' said Theo. 'Welcome to Sweet.'

Sarah looked him over for signs of the damage. His bad leg he held rigid, the ankle broken when she'd struggled with the weight of him on the hill path down to the car. From under the table the horns of his crutch stuck out. She remembered a dark shape on the white gravel, trying to pull itself up. Silently, like roadkill. Failing.

Then she said, 'Have you had lunch?'

'Sarah, it's three o' clock.'

'I think I might have something.' She realised she was rubbing her hands a little too much. The waitress appeared.

'Coffee please, and toast. Two pieces of brown toast, thank you.'

'That it?' the waitress said. Sarah couldn't look at her, she turned her face to the window and nodded lightly.

'What are you reading?' Outside the world was braced for more snow. Theo showed her the book cover. *The Last Man*, Mary Shelley.

'Oh,' Sarah said. Looking at his eyes. Downcast, feather-down eyes. 'I've read that,' she said. Theo lowered the book, and placed it on the table. She slid it over to her side, running her nails down the stiff glazed surface. It cracked like a yawning mouth when it opened. The coffee and toast arrived, and Theo had his cup refilled.

'It's interesting that you bought a new hardback copy of such an old book.'

'Tell me how it ends.'

'I might,' she said, 'but if I did I'd probably lie.'

'Sure there'd be plenty of reason to,' said Theo, holding his coffee cup near his mouth. Covert action, it made him seem to be flirting, almost. Did he know how he looked when he did that? He knew how to hold his shoulders with neither slackness nor stiffness. A small bump in his throat bobbed up and down as he drank; he sighed when he was finished.

'Why, Sarah?'

She tried to read his postures, but he was so well composed. And tried to think, again, what exactly were my motives, but really couldn't remember. So much thrummed between now and that point.

'I wanted to hurt something.' She could run, she could leave now, and not have to do this. She did not know how to do this. So folded her arms and looked down and carried on. 'To open something and ruin it. To open you up and hurt you.'

'Yes, you did that,' he said, looking into his coffee cup.

Sarah waited. Angry then. 'Why didn't you stop me?'

'Why didn't I stop you? I could have. You think I'm stronger than you. I am much stronger than you.'

'You are,' she said.

'I didn't stop you. Because I'm not strong, Sarah.'

He had held her wrists. Lying on insulator pelt and stones. Blood pump. Sarah kneeling. He hadn't pushed back. Open mouthed. The sky dark. Open throat. A radical vulnerability.

'And I hurt you. I kept hurting you. So strange—' Sarah stopped, unfolded her arms. 'Why didn't you tell anyone what I did?'

'Because I don't. Because I knew something was coming.'

'You knew something was going to happen?'

'I am not blind. It was all over you. You were boiling. I could have said no. To everything. I do regret the sex. Because it didn't feel right. I blame you. I blame myself. Neither of us are good people.'

He had practiced everything, but that was okay. He sat in the flickering spotlight and he said what he needed. Music played. A till opened and shut. The waitress tended to someone on the far side of the room. Footsteps clacked on their own shadows to keep them in place.

'I'm not even a person,' Sarah said quietly.

'Maybe not,' Theo said, 'grief does that.'

'I'm not grieving.'

Theo broke out a smile; faint, flat. He reached into his bag and pulled out something wrapped in newspapers.

'Your mom took this.'

It was a photo in a cedarwood frame. He pointed at the figures.

'Me, Gam. My brother Arturo. Arturo's wife Suzy, their daughter, Linn.'

Sarah touched the frame. Theo let her take it.

'Arturo died?'

'Arturo killed himself. After he came back from Iraq. After he killed Suzy. And after he killed my niece.'

'How long ago?'

'That doesn't matter.'

Theo moved his watch around on his wrist.

'I know I'm supposed to say something. But I can't,' Sarah said.

'Don't. Nobody can say anything that will make it all right.'

'Okay. Was it your fault? Why are you telling me this?'

'It was my fault,' Theo said. 'Nobody else to blame.' He turned the handle of his coffee cup. 'So, I knew about you. Who you were. What you did to your mom. Maud spoke about you a lot. To me, to Arturo. We'd drink in the woods while she painted. She always had wine around. She was great. So sharp,' here he looked off to his right, smiling, Sarah thought. 'Sharp, funny. But when she got more drunk and the painting wasn't going good, she would kind of screw up her eyes, and just stab the brush in the paint, not getting the colours right. Getting mad. Then she would start to rant. She told us the worst mistake in her life, that was you. That she loved you but you weren't really her daughter anymore.'

'Basic. Really basic. She could have—'

Theo looked at his hands. 'Yes, but it doesn't seem like she could.'

'When I came over for the first time. Did you know who I was?'

'It's why I didn't come down right away.'

He raised his head and looked out the window. Staring at an old man in a baseball cap slowly crossing the small car park in front of the café, walking away across the street, carrying a pile of towels. As he went the old man's legs kicked in an odd way, compensating for the snow.

'Where's he going to?' Theo murmured.

'To the hot springs?'

'He'd have to break in. They're closed today.'

'Because of the snow?'

'It's Christmas Eve, Sarah.'

Just as the words flowed out his mouth, Sarah had known the manner in which he would say her name. She wanted to say his name back at him, Theo, Theo, Theo, yes, yes. The two of them sat at the table. The winter outside. Existence was larger than any terrible thing. She ran her thumbnail around the lip of her cup.

'Is it really?' she said.

'Look,' Theo began.

'Theo,' she said, and all the words she could possibly say to him were clamped tightly together, so as not to rip from their seams and veins, 'I'm so sorry.'

Theo still faced the window.

'I think we should go outside.'

He stood and turned, showing her the back of his bent neck, the mass of hair above it thick, tumbling, he pulled on his coat and started hobbling away.

'You coming?' he said. 'Come on with me, quick.'

They went out to the entrance to the hot springs. The gate was wedged open. The chain had been cut.

'What's the plan, a swim?' Theo murmured. He didn't seem agitated. Sarah didn't know what he seemed. Stiff. He slittered through the gap and Sarah edged after. They stood in a courtyard made between two single-storey buildings and an adobe façade on the opposite side. The air was getting colder. Gasps of it were beginning to blow the old snow into drifts that reached high up the walls. In the centre of the courtyard there was an ornate tap above a black grated well. In summer mosses clung there, or trailing vines. Sarah read out the panel as they walked by.

'Arsenic-sulphur-iron-water for aid of digestion. Not Poisonous.'

'Look, don't. We've got to find this guy.'

'What do you think he's up to? Do you know him?'

'Yeah I know his face. At least I'm pretty sure. That's why I'm worried.'

'How far back does it go? Where are the springs?'

'Look—, just round the corner okay. Can you hear that?'

The sound of splashing. Through a door in the back wall. Tarp-covered rectangular pools, each about as big as a garden pond. Or a home pool, Sarah thought, though she'd never seen one. Steam wisped at their edges and each was separated by four-foot-high walls.

Theo and Sarah moved quickly from one to the next. It was the furthest from the door that was occupied. The tarp was pulled back and in the muddy water beneath there was a long, half-sunken shape, face down.

Sarah took off her coat and threw it on the snow as she ran. She pulled off her boots. The pool was four lengths of a body, about three as wide. There was a pile of clothes on the muddy, icy flagstones. She didn't stop. Into the hot, sloppy water. It covered her legs, it grasped her clothes. Shallow but it still came up to her shoulders. She leaned forward and grabbed at the human thing and pulled it towards the side. Theo helped her lift. A wave of mud flooded the sides. They rolled the body onto the ledge; a short, shirtless man with his features obscured by mud. No sign of breathing, though his whole body steamed. Theo reached for the stack of towels the stranger had brought, propped them under his head. Sarah found the drowned man's nostrils and cleared them.

'It's all right,' she said, 'it's all right.'

'I'll call an ambulance.'

The air was wet and freezing; the man's chest was still, or moving so faintly she couldn't tell.

'He's cold, we shouldn't move him. I'll be right back.' Theo limped off, leaving Sarah to vigil shivering. She reached into her pockets and scooped out a handful of mud. She put her hands on the man's oozy chest. To warm them, or just to have them there. Theo returned with dozens of towels, stolen from the reception.

'I called 911 on the landline. They say we need to keep him right here. Twenty minutes they think.'

Sarah helped him cover the man. They rubbed the towels over him, because what else could they do. They decided that he was breathing. He was still with them.

Theo stroked the man's head. The steam had gone from the body, and now a thin line of breath was visible. Sarah's teeth chattered. Fear and cold chatter. She wiped her mouth, tasting mud minerals.

'You see over by his towels?' asked Theo.

'No?'

There, on the rock, with the lid popped off was a tipped white bottle of Asprin, 200 count.

'Oh,' she said. She picked up the bottle and put it gently down beside the man.

'We'll tell them so they can pump his stomach. If they have to,' said Theo.

They heard the gates clang open. They shouted out.

Boots on snow. Crackle of radios. The stretcher was cranked flat. And the body straightened and lifted and taken up. A woman was talking to Sarah, guiding her through the courtyard with the black drain and the strange sign. She had not felt so wrecked in her body in a long time. But it didn't matter. All that did was for warmth and safety for the man. For the warmth of life. If it were possible. She and Theo were wrapped up in flimsy metallic blankets. The silver bent around Theo's face. His dark eyes wet. His crutches lost somewhere, his book. They got into the second ambulance together, sat on the seats a little apart. After a while, Sarah reached out to hold his hand.

96

The two of them sat in clean robes by Sarah's stove.

Sarah looked down the shadowy, flickering length of tweed blanket to the tips of her socked toes.

'Did he really want to die, you think?' Theo said.

'I don't know.'

'Christmas Eve,' he said. 'Why all the towels? Did he want to fool people? Hide the bolt cutters and pills?'

'I don't know,' Sarah said, 'we'll never get to know. You said his son died?'

'Yeah. Around the same time as Arturo was getting sent out.'

The fire clicked. Sarah pulled her knees up and hugged them.

'What dirty, fucked up years we've had to grow up in,' she said.

'I wouldn't call them any worse than anyone else's.'

'But I want to.'

She wanted to claim. She thought of endless valleys where the winds move for days at a time, full of the odour of the pine, the earth. Of rivers gleaming under the dead stars. Towns made out of signs. The more or less clean parcels of motel rooms. New York, who in its self-absorbed magnitude never loved her. What did she get to claim as her own? Where to go looking for somewhere clean, somewhere good?

The fire clicked again. Outside Sarah imagined a coyote howling, digging in frozen snow for a prairie dog burrow, or for some kind of shelter. But there was just the wind a little lost, scratching itself against the bark of trees.

'Hungry?' asked Theo.

'Yes, actually. Let's make something.'

A garlic and bread soup: they stood and ate spoonfuls from

the pot. When they got down halfway, Theo stepped back. He wiped his mouth. Sarah watched his eyes sweep the room. At last he seemed to shake whatever feeling was haunting him and spoke.

'This was – I'm going to say good. I don't know any other word. I don't have any more.'

'Me neither.'

He kissed her on the forehead. He struggled into muddy shoes.

'I can give you the robe later. Leave it for you on the porch.'

'If you like. You know, Gam's going to wonder where you've been all day,' Sarah said, laughing a little, just to help, if help was what he needed. 'I meant to ask, does she still hate me?'

'Yeah. But do you like her?'

'Honestly? No. Maybe admire her a bit.'

They stood at the door. Sarah hugged him around the waist. Everything was kind, for once. As soft as it could be. Theo leaned his head on her shoulder, then lifted it.

'And goodnight, Sarah.' Gently, with hard silver glints to his voice. But oh his eyes, oh the lines around his mouth. Once he had trudged far enough off into the blue dark Sarah turned the porch lights off.

97

You scramble with the beach bag, your voice crying like a seagull. Wait for me, Lucy! Mum, make her wait! The tide is receding over gleaming pebbles. With the light on your shoulder, and everything broad. Lucy shouts to you. Hurry up, why are you so slow? Lethargic, delicate, standing by the car putting on your swimming costume under a towel. A purity exists in the body of the girl you were, or in the memory. It spreads over everything like the morning.

You were crude and dirty and stupid, all of that, a hair trigger for rage, but on that day things were kinder. Your mum in an off-kilter mood. Her littleness wrapped in the tweed picnic blanket, smiling a private smile as she digs about in the car boot for the thermos and box of sandwiches. My darling pretty one, what will we do with you. Don't mind Lucy, if she gets to the sea before you, well. You'll just get a biscuit before she does. She hands you a mint Club and unwraps one for herself. You huddle round a cup of sugary tea, both watching Lucy, a gazelle, stride around cartwheeling the beach on her strong freckled legs.

Later you prod around in the mud, looking for razor shells. Mum says if you find any you can cook them up with shallots. You know that she won't help, that it will be Lucy who teaches you, if you do manage to pry any of those wormy white tubes from their burrows of silt. But Mum had still driven you here, and for that afternoon would be with you unconditionally. You are here. You remember and you are. This past moment still enacts in you a brightness, a seaside blistering cold.

Lucy has stripped to her navy bikini and is running for the waves and her hair runs like gold behind her. So you run too. The sun comes off the channel the colour of nostalgia. The yelps, the squeals, as first Lucy then you break the steel bands of the sea. Your teeth stop chattering. Lucy's hair strings in the wet, she screams at you to watch for another wave another and another, one after the other they hit you. Both of you shrieking, let the tide slam your sides, let the other girl tumble you over, splashing, yelling for joy. Your cousin might be your sister. Your life might be just like this all the time.

The figure of Maud at the shore. She slips off her sandals with difficulty and rolls up her coat. She has been ill, she has died. The beautiful, callous way she eyes the scene. Girls, I am going to join you.

Lucy and you shout back jeers. No way. Maud fumbles, she rolls off her tights. Her slow economical motions forbid denial of her sickness. The red scarf knotted around her head. You shouldn't come out, Mum, you call. You don't even have a bathing costume on. The sea mouths at her skirts. She keeps walking out to you until she has you in her arms. There, I told you. Don't ever doubt.

Lucy splashes the both of you. Aunt Maud, how on earth are you going to drive us back. Soaked to my knickers, Mum answers, grabbing her hand and pulling her niece close, making a group, a coven, slapping an armful of water over you all. Your mother has made a complete idiot of herself. You roll your eyes and work out how to get her back.

But in the dry portion of your head you think something like, I didn't think this would be fun, why is it so much fun, it's cold, oh fucking hell. And you are still astounded by how happy this always is. Three tiny figures strung together in the cool Atlantic swells.

Make it basic take it naïve So long Theo So long golden So long grass So long old road tracks heading uphill So long the scents of vanillin and juniper and the flowers whose names you never learned Goodbye Gam you fierce wrong person So long lavender stalks So long the garden you never planted and the greenhouse you killed Esta so long, So long the people you chose never to know So long plodding elk herds and the shepherding wind So long like a child waving from the back seat Goodbye knowing there is no end, and you straighten yourself freer under the rising sunlight painted on leaning mountains and you hope with weighted tenderness you will never see any of this again.

No houses near, no lights but pink stained sky, dimming the dawn star until it faded out. Sarah had driven all night and into the New Year. In winter the adobe houses look smaller. Abandoned homesteads by the side of the road like clay piggy banks cracked open, tagged with sad graffiti. Sarah stared out over the dash at the blacktop and listened to the satnav draw in a soft growl from northwest towards the south. She was nearing Albuquerque. All the land was desert. Sunshine now. Less scrub than near Santa Fe but still not the deserts she had in her head. The high sand dunes coloured white. Lizards manoeuvring their pale bellies up onto low rocks. Maybe those were Arabian, Australian deserts. Maybe they were New Mexican, but just not here.

There was a sign for a Native American casino and truck stop, and Sarah pulled in for some breakfast. She staggered out of the car on road legs. A feeling she enjoyed. Putting the work in to earn your fucking swagger, cashing the highway miles.

The diner of the truck stop was clean and laid out in red and white gingham. She sat down at the table closest to the door and ordered steak and eggs. This was sweet, this was good. Her fingers around the cutlery. The long braid of the waitress's hair. Black coffee. If Sarah had been a bad émigré, bad American, she had done it all due reverence in attention to the details. And now of this duty she divested herself. Foot by foot. She was going home.

What she would spend her money on

On renewal. An Englishwoman's home is a mansion, bounded by creek and cliff edge, black with ferns, with the narrow moon tapping at the slated roof. So the duty is: to make good, to earth wires, to prune hedges, to firm the knots, to dismantle stables or sand them, save them from the rot. But though she would sew the soil with raw cash, stuff the walls with premium ingredients (were they called ingredients, concrete, bricks, tiling, and the like?) it would not be for foxholing, not be for earthing herself.

Time keens to drag the walls of buildings down, and nature to cover the break with soil and seedlings. It is a strange urge we have to halt them, but there you go. We are a collective of strange urges, not even one of us more than ten per cent human in our mass of trembling cells, walking around in our embellishments, brushing up against one another and stinging, recoiling. It is our strange urge to take on projects. It is our strange urge to keep living. We spend our money when we have it. We try to know what harm it might do. So the duty is: to make something we hope is good. To work on something for years and then leave it for the public. The Warne as a picnic space. As a free artists' retreat. As series of high-ceilinged rooms all open, well-proportioned, ready to be passed through. To know that this might never happen. That all might come to no good at all. To work, to urge it on any way.

100

Before she drove to her motel, Sarah clipped a few more miles along the highway towards the Sandias mountains that flanked Albuquerque, dust-gold, snow-cased and pined. At some point the people of this city had built a road right to the top of the range. And it was essential that she follow that road while she was still here. Still American. Still with a need to fix some vista ahead of her, a landscape she could flood with her desires. But ask nothing from it, and leave it to its dry self.

The highway was extraordinarily pretty. Before the ascent, the square neighbourhoods ran by, held at a distance by a skirting of upmarket hotels and drive-and-park coffee houses and what might have been outlying college buildings all in harmonious earthenwork colours and shimmers of turquoise.

She drove with her shoulders down and back. Her hands firm. She had set everything in herself sparely. There was nothing more to say until the motel and after that the airport. She had told neither Theo nor Gam where she was going, but had begun planning the letter she would send from St Mawes. How much she would say, or justify of herself was difficult at this stage to judge. She would be creative with it.

Up and behind the mountains, the road looped. Ahead a single cyclist in blue lycra. Sarah slowed and the man saluted. He had a long steep way to go if she could judge correctly, and it was hard for Sarah to imagine powering to the top of a mountain, alone, in thin clothes. She wished him good deep lungs. At each loop the landscape grew colder. Snow thickened in the hollows under the conifers. Began to weigh on the branches and scale the trunks. There were some larger buildings glaring through the trees. One building or more than one. She had to keep her eyes on the winding of the road. She had to keep herself going before fatigue made her regret coming up. And now she had nearly a mile between herself and the cyclist, all that toil.

At the crest of the mountain was a car park and a visitors' centre. Sarah sat for a moment. She didn't need anything but the view. She got out and started walking for the centre anyway. On the fourth step up to the door, Sarah had to pause for breath. Her head hurt, and her chest. She bent over, which was a mistake. The blood sloshed around inside her skull until she straightened. She put her weight on the guardrail. This was some kind of attack. Mild, though. Her head whirred and tilted, but nothing unbearable.

Inside the visitor centre Sarah sought out a calm space, fingering some semiprecious stones in a jar. Letting them clatter turquoise pink down into their glass container. She drifted over to the corner of bookshelves and picked several candidates, on New Mexican history, birds of the Southern Rockies, wildflower guides. The wooze continued. She tacked about from one side of the shop to the other.

A poster on the wall with a picture of the peaks on a summer day read Sandia Crest, NM. 10,678 feet above sea level. That couldn't be right. How could they be so high? Then she remembered, Albuquerque, NM was already five thousand feet above sea level. Meaning that Sarah had just driven up an additional five k very fast and had given herself altitude sickness. Felt like being trashed. With this information, it still took her twenty minutes to decide what to do. She practised breathing in, breathing out. She looked at Native American jewellery. Picked up a toy bluebird. Pressed the button to hear its call. She looked the display of birds up and down. The only right course of action was for her to take a moment to pinch each and every button. A forest of electronic chirping and hoots burst out. Sarah listened to the chorus, wincing. After the chirrekawreeps wore off, she went outside, over to the edge of the mountain.

She stood on the overlook and gazed out over a white tree-speckled ridge down to the sprawl of Albuquerque and the plains beyond it. They looked to be plains, to be golden like the grass of the valley. The buttress of the mountain range seemed from above built to hold back an evident tide. Clouds were casting mile-square shadows over the enormous urban landscape, over a city built so low that from this height it seemed more like a map than a real place.

But that was only one way of looking at it. To another person, it would be a city with memories hitched. Theo would think; that was my apartment over there. There, the library. He'd know the downtown and a good place to go swimming in the summer. Sarah didn't need a guide. And for one night's worth of it, Albuquerque would be her city too.

She drove down off the mountain and grounded herself in one last motel. White sheets. A documentary about Alaskan bears. These conclusions for America: a firm bed, a hot and slightly worn-out shower. The ice machine murmuring downstairs.

101

Albuquerque. Newark. Heathrow.

Sarah was somewhere over the Midwest eating a brown bread roll when she thought of the Sixth Street garden which had been out of mind forever. Strange to think of it now. Evenings when Kennedy had come in her pussy-bow dress and her blonde hair, how she had pressed her kisses against Sarah's lips until they felt scalded. Nights when the foreign hotel sheets would encase them in a single silk cocoon. Now Sarah's memories felt cool and stable and Kennedy had become a woman the days had divided. Simplified like a story told. Perhaps that was how New York would work for her. As a made-up place that she could contain in certain instances, and let the rest crumble away.

Outside of the Sixth Street garden beyond the high gates was the city; the stones and pavements and other tiny parks set in patches of stolen greenery. The people underground and high above it, threading, slouching, muttering. Dirty, awful, charming, successful New Yorkers. And then putting edges to the city, the rivers, and the sea. The city was like a row of sandcastles and for her the tide was coming in. A sandcastle is never destroyed, it just falls back into soft damp sand. On a different day, in another summer, some other child will come along and build the grains back up into a world as they see it.

The meal tray was removed and Sarah closed her eyes. She thought of all the states she would never visit. Arizona, California. The Pacific Northwest where they said it rained all the time and had forests of red monster trees enduring long and silent lives. Unmolested by salt magic. She thought about rocks keeping the continent in place, and of black lakes cuffed by snow. About guns and broken down bits of cities where the weeds grow and there is no place to get a warm meal.

Her list was too simple. And all this is a beach. In short, she thought about America until America became kinder and more edgeless. She thought kindly of it as it faded away. She rested her head against the seatback and listened to the murmur of passengers behind her. None of America was hers, she had failed. But if you think about it in another way, it's true that the shore belongs only to itself and to its sea.

102

'You could be on Browne family land for a mile and not know it,' the taxi driver said, 'old family. How do you know them?' After they got to the turn he wouldn't take Sarah down the steep flagstone road that ran through the pasture. So she got out there and walked with her luggage, in her camel-coloured winter coat. There were ravens at roost in the yews and the shadows of memory, wheeling and calling.

The brickwork wall came round in front of the house forever and always. A pair of stone owls gazed down at her as she stood watching the lights of the house through the open gate. Lucy had come ahead to take off the sheeting, and so that they could discuss the renovations and non-salvageable areas. A bit had been done in Maud's latter years, preventative measures, really. Hampered by indecision, the tumescence of the cancer through bone marrow. Hampered by a lack of daughter there to hold her hand. Sarah touched her hair. Her bags swung against her. You're still a small person, charging downhill in the cold.

Aunt Selene was off working and would not come all the way from Bristol. What more could be expected? Next Christmastime, maybe Sarah would put on a good show of welcome. Not even wicked aunts last forever. Well, she might. But anyway, Lucy was inside waiting for her like a figure of parable. She had helped arrange things voicelessly, by email, by text. I'll be waiting for you, however late you get in. I'll make us dinner, how does that sound? There it was, sheared of tone. How does it sound? Nothing to indicate. Nothing of the pain. It had been four years since they'd met, briefly, in London. There was no way to tell who the woman was now. But balanced, probably, the way she'd been a practical teenager co-habiting a bold wreck of a house, with two drunks and a scowling girl she'd had to teach to feed herself. And pick up off the floor when the adults had been particularly nasty. Lucy would be in the library, reading non-fiction, having put the lamps on right when it started to turn dark, because she knew her guest would want the light.

Sarah could see the corner window of the library that faced the northern lawn. It made sense that Lucy would be in there, if it was still the warmest and driest room. Should she go in the front way? More a guest or a strange event. She chose the back, following the wall, following the textures of lichen and chipped grouting, or whatever it was called. She roughed her hand up on it. But not so rough that it skinned her.

The sign for the walled garden was just as it needed to be. Sleek new ivy hung listlessly over the arch.

Seedpods of poppies and five-footer hemlock stalks. Where was this, it had ceased to be reality. Sarah walked along the path on a tightrope. Her throat constricting further with each step, her eyes squinting to see ahead in the dimness. Someone had tied the long roses back so now their briars did not block the way. When you are young, you think everyone more or less has the life you have. Even if you know not every house is this one: elegant frontage, empty rooms, fish and slimy pools, and the lights of passing tankers. And for her it had been a stage and she could see no curtain and there was no good metaphor clever enough to describe it.

Sarah waited. The immense house stood, with one light visible on the lower floor. It seemed a place without calluses. And who was she coming back to it, at last? A perpetrator, mesh of images and conclusions. Girl-monster, beloved daughter, in the dark.

Sarah put her hands on the worn green door to the house – unlocked, because there was nothing much inside the house to steal and it had been waiting for her – and pushed it inwards. She took some deep breaths of chilly clammy salt-stained night air. The door creaked all the way wide. And in she walked through, backed by the blackout shapes of trees and the mass of petrified flowerbeds.

Acknowledgements

First of all, my dearest thanks to Douglas Dunbar for accompanying me on the research trips to both New Mexico (two and half days straight on the Greyhound bus, much driving, camping and the beauty, heat and chill of the high desert) and to Cornwall, and for our life together in New York, and all of it after, and for his thoughts and critique on the book as it struggled into being. To Susan Estes and Dr. Bob Parmenter for their invaluable information given so long ago now on the lives of elk of the Valles Caldera, New Mexico and for the detail that the Spanish accent in the area has the Castilian lisp – any interpretation I have made of their answers is entirely my doing. Thanks to my mother and father, for their unwavering support (and the childhood trips to Cornwall), and to Ann, Thom, Nicki, and David for their efforts on the other side of the Atlantic. Thanks to my friend Jimmy, who told me this book would be hard to publish (and he was not wrong). Gratitude, therefore, to Freight Books for doing so: to Adrian Searle and Robbie Guillory and Laura Waddell and especially to the sharp-eyed and astute Vicki Jarrett for her edits. Thank you to Jenny Brown, and The Saltire Society, and Creative Scotland. And to the Glasgow CW PhD cohort for ongoing moral support. Thank you to CCM press, Sundog Lit, Necessary Fiction (hello Steve!) and *3:AM* magazine for publishing excerpts of the novel.

Once again, and finally – to the unlikeable women.